HEALER'S QUEST

Jessica Palmer

Cover illustration by David Wyatt

SCHOLASTIC

Scholastic Children's Books,
Scholastic Publications Ltd,
7–9 Pratt Street, London NW1 0AE, UK

Scholastic Inc.,
730 Broadway, New York, NY 10003, USA

Scholastic Canada Ltd,
123 Newkirk Road, Richmond Hill,
Ontario, Canada L4C 3G5

Ashton Scholastic Pty Ltd,
P O Box 579, Gosford, New South Wales,
Australia

Ashton Scholastic Ltd,
Private Bag 1, Penrose, Auckland,
New Zealand

First published by Scholastic Publications Ltd, 1993

ISBN 0 590 55428 X

Typeset by TW Typesetting, Midsomer Norton, Avon
Printed by Cox & Wyman Ltd, Reading, Berks.

10 9 8 7 6 5 4 3 2 1

For Brendan, Michael, Lisa and Emily
– and Steve too –
this flight of fancy.

Author's note:

Welcome to Renegades World, where earth elementals make ponderous progress across the face of the map, fire dances in human form and air elementals drift like dust upon the wind. An Appendix has been supplied for those who want to know more about this place where universes meet and merge.

MORTAL PLANE
N
Realm of Snow Elves
SZATMAR
FIRTH
EUBONIA
THE NORTHERN CONTINENT
Principality of Merovnick
Great Northern Wastes
NORVON
SHALOP
URI
Realm of Sea Elves
River Ullr
Greybeard Tor
LAVANTHIA
City States Of
TICINO
Abruzzi
Thessalia
DAKLHA
THE SOUTHERN CONTINENT
Pelopnos
Isle of Learning
ABDHA
Serpetine River
HAMADAN
Miasmic Swamp
Al Khali
QUATTARA
SHAMIR
Important Stone Circles Marked:
CARTOGRAPHY BY D·WYATT · FROM EXPLORATIONS BY J·PALMER ·93·

Prologue

Astra Aurelius slipped out from under the sleeping man. The air elemental was no more than a wisp – a mere whisper of a woman. Small enough to fit into the palm of one's hand, to the human eye the Lady Astra appeared little more than a picture etched in glass. A smile flickered across translucent lips as water chuckled musically down the fountain, and her fluid cousins sang their joy. The air elemental hugged herself, did a joyous jig, and a whirlwind whipped around the reclining form and the dancing vision.

She was with child.

Somewhere behind her a voice shrieked in

triumphant scorn. The scream retreated rapidly, becoming indistinct. The haunting cry shivered up her spine. The frolicking sprite faltered and frowned.

What was that?

The spinning clouds of fairy dust settled around her. Her normally quicksilver thoughts bogged down, and the fountain's chords fell flat, striking a sour note. Below her flickering image, the man's skin had taken on a blue-grey hue, and Astra forgot all else.

This would never do.

The man was real – this mortal man with his hard lips and soft touch – and he might perish if not returned to mortal realm soon. For man was a thing of earth, and he needed to be rooted in time and place, to have solid soil beneath his feet, in order to survive. Here in this portal between the planes, far beyond earth's stodgy realm, all times merged. Past, present and future became one. For a mortal to tarry here was dangerous. He would most assuredly die if he remained inside the stone circle overlong.

The lady extended a wavery arm to caress the raven head. To bring him here had taken powerful magic, and already she could feel her energies starting to drain.

Her scowl of concentration deepened. There was something she should remember and couldn't. Something to do with the fleeing cry. Some reason why she must linger here, and some reason why she should not whisk her all-too-human lover back to the security of the earthly plane.

Astra shook her head and the thought was lost, dispersed like smoke on the summer breeze. Without further deliberation, the fairy clothed herself in cobwebs and wrapped her gauzy form in mist so that she could not be seen by prying mortal eyes. Then she embraced her beloved – whose name she could no longer recall – and shrouding him also in her protective haze, the elemental passed through the portal into the earth plane. They reappeared, another ripple among the many heat waves that radiated off the scalding hot sands of the Shamirian desert.

Wicked laughter echoed about the vacant circle, and a figure materialized out of thin air. The form was flat and two-dimensional, like a man made of twigs. The picture wobbled uncertainly for a moment.

For hundreds of thousands of rotations, the wizard had been trapped between planes, caught like a black-moss fly on sticky paper and pressed flat. Released, he had yet to regain mass or bulk, so when he turned sideways he appeared little more than a line. Faced head on, his image was stretched thin like paint on canvas.

The mage paced, or tried to pace, but the best he could manage was something between a swaying stagger and an energetic hobble. His imprisonment had broken his body but not his mind, for the wizard swore spiritedly as he lurched from one end of the stone circle to another.

Once his power had been such that it had taken the entire Council of Wizards to defeat him, and then, as if they thought no more of him than a troublesome gnat, the magicians had given him over to be guarded by that silly, flitting elemental.

The Lady Astra, queen of her kind, had been perfect for the job. She would not listen to his blandishments. No elemental could be swayed by power or wealth, for all the fay folk had magical skills that exceeded that of the mages on the mortal plane. The lady's head could not even be turned by wizardly promises of immortality, for she was already immortal. And as for money!

The earth elemental would simply take a gold coin back to its earthen breast from where it came. The water elemental would wear it down with its liquid play. Fire would melt it, while air might be attracted by its sheen, so like that of the sun, but would quickly forget it, leaving it behind as soon as something else took her fancy.

Air, who protected man's plane from water and fire, was the natural choice. Her earthy cousins had the memory of the fabled furry mammoth of the Northern Wastes, but were so slow that it took them turns to complete a thought much less an action. Her watery cousins had more flexibility than earth, but were confined in beds of streams, or bowls of lakes. Fire, the only element ever to be harnessed by mankind, was considered corruptible.

Queb had been well and truly stuck until the mortal had stumbled on the scene, distracting her. For the airy sprite had wit, freedom of movement and quickness aplenty, but the memory of a sieve, and that had been her weak point.

Bless her empty head! He threw back his head and cackled gleefully, a sound like the scraping of nails across a chalkboard.

A single drooping eye gazed upon the hated fountain. The red orb burned with Brimstone's fire. The water began to seethe and churn, and the fountain simpered pathetically. The twisted, nearly toothless mouth sneered as a skeletal arm waved at his reflection in the pool. The water started to bubble and boil, and the central statue split with a loud crack.

Calmly, the necromancer told himself. He had time. Plenty of time. Fairy babes come when and where they will, in the blinking of an eye or in many turns of the planets. But once the child was born, it would be subject to the same mortal calendar as its father was.

The sorcerer had time to strengthen himself, to plan, to prepare to wreak his revenge on the Lady's whelp. Her birth was an abomination, and with her elemental blood undiluted by time, the child was the only one on the mortal plane who could possibly rival his power. But Queb could achieve no more as long as he was lumbered with this useless shell.

And the apparition vanished, shouting a single word: *Free-e-e-e-e!*

CHAPTER 1

The Matriarch of Healers moved silently in the inner sanctum of the college. Housed in a giant dome-like greenhouse, the walls and roof were constructed of carved crystal that caught the light and sent it tumbling out in a myriad of tiny rainbows. Even at night, by the light of the three visible moons, the herbarium was a riot of colour, and the sweet scent of medicinal herbs permeated the still, damp air.

With minute slivers of crystal and amethyst woven into the cloth, her robes of office shimmered with each nervous movement. Exquisitely wrought chains adorned the woman's wrists and ankles, and hanging from each golden link was a tiny chime which pealed tremulously with her restless motion. The priestess peered into the agitated waters of the crystal pond, her eyes seeking its heart, but the normally clear waters were black, the rainbow colours devoured in the swirling umbra. With a sharp inhalation, the Matriarch reached out and touched the cool water in Brigitta's sacred pool.

Its roiling surface calmed and a picture emerged – a man who wore the faded robes of a wizard. His face was borne of nightmare and it was old, centuries old. Crêpe paper skin, marred by pox and covered in oozing sores, hung loosely on an elongated skull, but the head was inclined slightly away so the Matriarch could not quite see the eyes. As she noticed this, as if suddenly aware that he was being observed, he swung round. A single fiery eye fixed on the priestess's face, holding her spellbound. It bored deeply into her psyche. With terrific effort, the woman lifted her hand to place it between herself and the glaring, baleful eye, breaking the thrall, and the image burst like a bubble.

Trembling, the priestess backed away from the pond. She recognized him as one they had thought long-since dead. And the Matriarch wondered if the mirror showed her what had already passed or something which was yet to be.

The Lady Astra flitted around the empty glen, searching. She'd explored every cranny and nook from velvet green floor to graceful bough and beyond to the top of the hoary rocks. She'd lifted leaf and twig and peered under every blade of grass, not once or twice, but many times. On bended knee, the lady peered hopefully under a clover and then rocked back on her heels and sighed.

"Gone!" she cried out loud, and her voice rattled across the circle like autumn leaves rustling in a stiff breeze.

Behind her, the water elementals worked furiously to repair the fountain and sculpt it, incorporating the crack into the design. Yet there was something forlorn about the reshaped structure. Although her watery cousins still frolicked and sang, their melody had changed, switched to minor chords as if they had absorbed the sorrow that weighted Astra's fairy spirit until she was as slow and sluggish as her earthy relations.

The elemental sagged, tiny shoulders drooped. If she could only remember what she was looking for! Astra rifled through hazy memory. It was something dark and deadly, and as doleful as the dirge the water elementals now sang; something she wasn't really sure she wanted to find; a trust the lady had been given as queen of her kind and then lost.

Dimly the Lady Astra recalled her downfall. A man, a mortal man, and later a child. Yes, a daughter – and despite herself, the fairy smiled. A wee bairn by mortal standards, but far too large for Astra to keep, so sadly the elemental had returned it to its sire.

Many turns had passed in mortal time, but here in air's domain, it had been little more than an instant, so Astra bent once more to her search and poked at a flower to see what it hid within its folds.

The wizard shuffled across the room, a flask in his hand. The cavern was hewn out of solid rock, deep in the belly of a great mountain. Around him tables were scattered, and upon each lay a covered human form. Many of the figures were misshapen, deformity visible even through the thick blanket. Others were straight and true, though small and shrunken.

One was exposed, the cover thrown aside to reveal a featureless face. Queb stared impassively down on the homunculus. A creature of magical creation, and another one of his many failed experiments. This one he would let live.

It wasn't too repugnant. It was *almost* human, near perfect in form, albeit a trifle small. A man in miniature. Except of course for the blank where the face should be, without eyes, nose or mouth.

Queb had fled the second plane immediately, lest he be caught there once he had attained three dimensions, but it had taken ages for his body to swell. Even now his figure was wraith-thin, and he knew that though his powers were great, he could accomplish little shackled with this shell. So he experimented, trying to make a new body to house his raging spirit.

The wizard swirled the amber fluid in the flask pensively, wondering where he had gone wrong. His concentration was such that he didn't notice the sudden appearance of the old crone in the mirror, but he felt her eyes upon him before he understood their source. He pivoted, and his jaw unhinged. The small flask slid from nerveless fingers and crashed to the stone floor, exploding with a bang. Shards of glass flew everywhere, embedding in some of the shrouded forms and, strangely, drawing blood, but Queb's eyes were trained on the unannounced spectre. He glowered at her, taking in the elaborate headdress and the long robes which, if he used his imagination, were reminiscent of the simple gown of the healer. Had the healers also yielded to pomp and show like the wizards? It seems a sad state of affairs had developed since he had once been Archmage.

Their gazes locked, and the woman froze. The two wills battled for a minute, but the woman was stronger than most. She lifted her arm slowly, as if it were a struggle to do so, and placed her hand over her eyes, breaking the binding that he tried to weave about her. Then, just as quickly as she came, she was gone.

The wizard moved too as though released from a spell. He pondered this woman whose image arose unbidden in his looking glass to man's world. A healer? He had had little time for healers in the past. He had less time for them now. Unless . . . they could rid him of this inhospitable shell.

Her will had been strong, but he could tell that she was not quite strong enough. Had she not surprised him, she would never have escaped his clutches, and Queb could manipulate her if he chose to. If he was careful. If he was subtle. He filed her face away for future reference. She might be useful to him some day.

Tilting his head to one side, he wondered who or what had brought her here. What did her appearance portend?

Behind him a figure sat up, the cover falling away to expose a creature with two faces, one on either side of its head. It spoke, and the wizard jumped. Glass dug a deep slice through his slipper to his foot, but his body was so desiccated and dry that he hardly noticed.

"*I* brought her to you," spoke a deep and resonant voice that came not from either mouth, but from deep within the belly. "Your search draws to a close."

Queb cocked his head, listening intently, for it seemed he recognized those fell tones. The Devil, The King of the Darklands, Archfiend. He had been foolish enough to invoke this particular demon during that final battle.

The voice reverberated inside the wizard's skull, and images of death, destruction and disease popped into his mind. The mage's heart clapped wildly in his chest.

"What search?" he said cagily, for it did not pay to let the Devil know too much of one's plans.

"What search, indeed. You would play games with me? I who came to you once long ago? You owe me!"

The ancient mage waved his hand with airy abandon. "I have dealt with many of Hades' devils in my time. Which one are you?"

"Hah, mortal! You know. Besides, who I am does not matter. What matters is that I've chosen to help you. I grow weary of this dark domain and have come now for payment of past services," it chuckled unpleasantly.

The wizard's paper-thin heart did a quick trot around his ribcage.

"If you must identify me, you shall know me by my mark: pestilence and plague." And the body went limp, folding like an empty bladder.

"Wait a second!" Queb said. The eyes popped open. "What should I call you?"

"For now, you can call me friend," the voice twittered wickedly.

"Then how should I call you? Get in touch with you, I mean," Queb added.

"*You* don't call *me; I'll* call *you*." The figure was lifeless once more.

All the following day, the high priestess of Brigitta worried and fretted. The sun set and the first moon peeked over the horizon as she paced next to the now silent pond. By the time night fell, the Matriarch decided she must act.

Her slippered footsteps resounded loudly across the empty marble forecourt as she hastened towards the Wizards' College. The guard owl erupted from the branches of a tree the moment she entered the gate. Acting as messenger it took wing, flying to inform the wizards of her approach.

Her stride was so fast that her skirts flew out

before her. Her rigid back and stern countenance revealed her displeasure. She moved not as a meek supplicant, but with a confident step befitting the one who was the Crown of Brigitta.

The Matriarch hated the Wizards' College. It was so cold and impersonal, like its occupants the wizards. The once white building had been sullied, having turned the sulphurous yellow of magic. Gargoyles and other fantastical creatures had been added to the structure – ridiculous things meant to intimidate those who sought answers here. In this, too, the imposing edifice reflected its inhabitants, more interested in the vestiges of authority than in its responsibilities.

Pounding on the massive door, the Matriarch chafed at the restriction the wizards had imposed on magic. The Wizards' Guild held sorcery's reins fast and seized secular power that eclipsed even that of the kings of the northern continents and the sheiks and sultans of the southern domain. They clutched their prerogative greedily, controlling the lives of the people and withholding magic and its use from all but a chosen few.

Most were barred from entry into the Sorcerers' Guild. The list included all women, and any peasant, freeman or merchant – unless they came with glittering coin. The wizards would not accept the clay markers of the common man. Only fat gold Pentacles – more money than most people would see in a lifetime of hard labour – would satisfy their greed. Even gold in hand was not enough, for a recommendation from someone highly placed was deemed necessary. This excluded just about everyone except sons of guild members and lesser sons of nobility whose abilities and purse permitted such an education.

Any found practising magic without the proper certificate and licences were burned as heretic and witch. Heretics because the wizards in their pride claimed all gods as their own, and witch because all magic outside guild control was witchery. Even illusionists, whose paltry tricks were the entertainment of the masses, were condemned to the stake unless they could prove that they had proper licences, certificates and degrees, and guild tax, paid in full.

The Matriarch marched back and forth across the broad porch. She knew they kept her waiting on purpose. This was one of their many subtle ways of putting her in her place, for the Healers' Guild was separate – a maidenly craft and a poor cousin to the sorcerers. All agreed that the source of healing was magic, but the healers' craft was considered one more suitable for the fairer sex. Even men must forswear their gender when they entered the guild. When they joined they became one of the castrata.

The nail-studded door creaked open, and a frightened apprentice appeared, bobbing and bowing and bid her enter with a wave of his hand. She announced her intention, and he scurried off.

"Curse the man!" she muttered. They would make her wait longer still. The Matriarch quashed her indignation, for healers lived on people's good will, especially that of the wizards. They were not permitted to exact payment for their treatments, but depended on donations for their support, and their accounts were administered by the wizards since it was thought that women had not the wit for maths.

"A pox on them!" she muttered. The Matriarch had little patience for the system which kept the healers close to penury, and she particularly despised the wizards who administered it. Now they left her cooling her heels in the vestibule – another way of indicating their superiority.

Only the healers' status as a religious sect kept them independent of the wizards. Hidden under the mantle and protection of Brigitta, a woman could practise this small sorcery with the wizards' blessing, although the Matriarch often suspected that it was perhaps the craft itself that was the deciding factor. Sorcerers were conspicuously absent when there was even a whisper of disease. These stalwart males, and self-proclaimed protectors of the lesser healers, vanished with the first appearance of bloody flux or plague.

As clerics, they were kept cloistered, separated from the people whom they would serve. What patients they had came to them in their temples and their halls, and this too angered the Matriarch. Healers should be out there, administering to the sick and the poor and not leaving their treatment to the village witch.

A draught blew throughout the hall. The old codger was trying to goad her but she must not let him. The Matriarch genuflected, hands crossed, fingers waggling, unconsciously performing the flap-wing sign of the dove.

The message she carried was too important to let one ill-tempered conjurer get under her skin. She inhaled deeply in a *pranayama*, a prayer of breath.

There was a ripple of movement, and the Archmage Philos the Benevolent swept down the long hall, his staff clacking hard against the stone floor, revealing his irritation.

Why they called him benevolent, the Matriarch didn't know. He had a permanently sour expression and he hated women in general and the Matriarch in particular. His feeble attempts to assert his authority reminded the priestess more of a petulant child than an archmage, ruler of magic and therefore overlord of peasant and king alike. Often she wondered if he had been deprived of sweets or a mother's love as a child. For who but a mother could have loved him? And she must have been hard-pressed to do so!

With a blast of magic that echoed like a clarion call inside the Matriarch's trained ear, Philos the not-so-benevolent swooped into the entry chamber, dressed as usual in the tastelessly ornate blue-black robes of his craft.

"What is it that is so urgent that you must interrupt my tea?" he said.

The Matriarch bowed her head to hide her fury. At this hour her healers lay abed, compelled into keeping peasants' hours by the wizards' miserly nature. For as well as keeping the healers' accounts, the wizards were also in charge of supplies. They doled out lamp oil, keeping the healers in short supply so that their own tapers and lanterns could glow late into the night. They didn't seem to care that their "little sisters" must keep the infirmary lit at all times. By ancient writ, found only in magical scrolls, the healers were given no oil to light their lamps during the dark days of the five moons, and had to save what they obtained during the moons' fullnesses. The reasons for this were lost in the mists of time.

But the Wizards' College always blazed with light. They luxuriated in a late tea, after a leisurely dinner, while the healers tightened their belts. The Matriarch wished fervently that the Archmage would choke on his repast and then suppressed the thought as unworthy of her.

"Are we to talk here," she asked, "where the walls have ears?"

As if in answer to a summons, two large ears sprouted from either side of the room.

Magic was not natural to humanity, for it had seeped into the earth plane from the others where it belonged. Many believed that magic had a mind of its own, and even the best sorcerers could scarcely control it. It took the strongest of wills to summon sorcery on demand, and its use required an outlay of power that drained its user.

The sorcerer could send forth his spirit to roam free or to inhabit the body of a lesser being, but it was a dangerous thing to do. The Matriarch herself had witnessed the procedure – had seen the cord that had tied the human body to the recipient – and she knew with a healer's instinct that to sever the cord between the two would be to sever the life of both.

In a place like the college, spells often got loose and would run amok until someone could master them, at least temporarily, and confine them. A poorly aimed enchantment could ricochet and rebound upon its maker, turning him into a toad, or it could hit walls or floor, and be absorbed by them so that they would sprout ears on demand.

Benevolent raised a hoary brow, considered the wiggling ears and hissed his agreement. "Yes, perhaps we should go somewhere a little more private."

He led the Matriarch down the hall into an antechamber. With broad gestures of his gnarled hands, he checked the room for eaves-droppers, magical or otherwise, and a charm concealed somewhere in the shadows yipped and dashed out into the light.

"Hmph!" the wizard mumbled. "Most likely a leftover of some young prankster. Begone!"

The priestess had to cover her mouth with her hand to hide her smile as the dislodged talisman ran screeching from the chamber. Like magic, charms and talismans had some small part of the beings that made them. For example, a fire wand contained the magic of the fiery elemental. As such, these things were stubborn and always yearned for their former home. They would disappear and reappear on a whim, escaping to the elemental planes from whence they came.

Time differed there, where a minute could be an hour or an hour a minute. For the mage, this could have dire consequences if an essential piece of equipment vanished during a spell – only for a moment in the elemental plane – never to return until after the death of the original owner. This could be a little difficult for the new owner, who might look down one day and suddenly discover that a wand had landed with a plop right into the middle of his soup.

The Archmage glared after the skittering enchantment and harrumphed. "That was the last of it, I believe. This room is safe."

The Matriarch nodded. "Do you remember Queb?" she asked.

"Of course I remember Queb. Not a bairn is born that hasn't heard: 'Queb'll get you if you don't watch out,'" the Archmage replied. "What wizard could forget the dark times when the Archmage turned to evil and upset the balance between planes? The battle nearly killed half our people, and it was years before the people trusted us again."

"After the battle, what did you do with him? With his powers, surely he couldn't be allowed to go free? And with his skills, where could you keep him?"

"That, my good Mother, is a trade secret." He glowered at her and sniffed disdainfully. "What did we do with him, indeed!"

"It's important that I know."

"Well, if I remember correctly, he was banished between the planes. Since he sought to upset the balance, it seemed a fitting punishment."

"Then you didn't kill him?"

"Madam, we are wizards not necromancers. We value life as much as any healer does."

"I feared you would say that."

"Why? Why this interest in something now thought of as a children's fable? Few outside this institution realize that Queb ever existed, although the legend is still told. Most use it as a tale to terrify toddlers."

"He still exists." It was a statement, not a question.

"Unlikely," the Archmage said.

"Unlikely, perhaps, but true, for I saw him. I fear that he is loose and ready to take revenge on those who banished him."

The air between them crackled.

"It could not be!" Benevolent said. "He's dead. He must be. He has to be, after all this time. He was vanquished, banished after the battle many turns ago."

"I tell you I saw him with my own eyes."

The Archmage lifted his arms, clenched and unclenched his fists, and sparks flew between them. The priestess took an involuntary step backwards. She had not expected this reaction, and secretly she wished she could threaten him in kind, with a flash of magic and a childish display of temper. "And how did you see him with your own eyes?" he demanded.

"He came to me in a . . . vision."

"What vision is this? If I did not know you for the Matriarch, and Crown of Brigitta, I'd scream heresy. You are supposed to be above the petty temptations of mortal womanly witchery. If I did not know every little wrinkle upon your face, I'd say you were some changeling."

The Matriarch's mouth clapped shut, for she knew she had some small magic of her own, beyond healing. Even before joining the order, she had been able to predict the gender of an unborn child or recognize magic and the true magician when she saw them.

Additional skills came with her elevation to Matriarch, skills she shared with her chosen second. The gift of sight in the Pond of Brigitta was one such skill. It was a well-kept secret, for not even the wizards had this gift of far-seeing, and in this world, the seer was the most hunted heretic of all. Each Matriarch lived in fear that she would someday grace the stake.

The woman frowned under her cowl of woven crystal. The priestess's powers were puny, goddess-inspired, and the Matriarch was too old and tired to fight the system. That task would be left for her successor. She could not argue against the charge of witchery, and even someone as high as she could be convicted.

"It came to me in the Dream Fields. Since it concerned a wizard, *the* Wizard, I thought I should tell you," she finished lamely.

"Why should I concern myself with womanly hysteria? Dream Fields! Fantasy's fields, more likely. An old woman's nightmares. Pah!" He threw his hands up in exasperation.

"A message from . . . Brigitta. A warning. As her messenger, I should know." She raised her head and the elaborate headdress to its full height.

"Brigitta's warning for us? And what interest does Brigitta's chosen have in the workings of man's magic?" he purred, and she saw the trap hidden amongst his words.

"Nothing," she murmured. "Nothing at all."

Seeing her sufficiently cowed, the Archmage softened slightly. "Bring me proof and then we can talk." He turned on his heel and strode from the room, his staff clack, clack, clacking as he went down the hall. She had been dismissed.

The high priestess made no further attempt to hide her fury. She spat a curse after him and then she too spun in a clatter of crystal and marched out of the door.

The fog, a nightly visitor, had crept over the Isle of Learning, and the Matriarch's footsteps were muffled and muted. The mist cooled her flushed skin as she skirted the circle of stones that marked the boundary between the Wizards' College and the Healers' Temple. She was only vaguely aware of it as she passed. A circle within a circle within a circle, really, although one could hardly tell from the outside. But the priestess had seen the original plans, drawn upon the wall in the Archmage's office which by right should be hers. There were nine stones in the outer ring, representing each of the nine planes, followed by two staggered circles of seven, for the gods and their planets. The inner ring consisted of five stones, one for each of the moons, and at its heart a single megalith towered above the rest, a symbol of the One that binds all together.

A patch of fog slithered from behind a stone and drifted after her. Under closer scrutiny, the flitting shade became a person who moved with an almost unnatural silence. Not a blade stirred nor a pebble rattled. Even the fog seemed to accept this strange spectre unquestioningly.

The apparition stalked the jingling cleric. Occasionally the woman would stop and sputter, and the shade paused too. As she entered the outer vestibule, it halted and hovered, a piece of the night that melted into the shadows on the temple doorstep.

Proof, he said he wanted. Proof he would get, but how?

The Matriarch went back to stare at the pond and consider.

Since the rape of Brigitta by the war god, Og – when it had been proved that the Divine Mother could be taken like any other puling female – the sisterhood had lost strength. Before that time, all had bent the knee to the Sacred Mother. The ravishment of Brigitta had meant the downfall of the healers. The healers' loss had been women's loss, and now they were little more than cattle, things with which men could haggle and barter. A woman's body could be exchanged for land or power and daughters discarded as useless or bought and sold for a pitiful few clay markers. It was said that only when man and woman walked as equals and dwelt as partners, shoulder to shoulder and hand in hand, would Brigitta again be raised to Her former glory.

Meanwhile the pool played the same scene over and over again. The Blessed Brigitta was trying to tell her something – something she should notice, something she should see. Her eyes lit on the bell, hanging around the acolyte's neck.

"Ah," she said, and a plan began to form in her mind.

A piece of darkness separated itself from the mist-shrouded door. The shade wore a heavy cloak of indiscriminate colour, ranging from grey to black, and designed in such a way that its wearer would blend into his surroundings. A slender hand extended from between the folds to push back the hood and reveal the startling silver hair of the snow elf.

The form shifted to rest a pale fist on his hip, and the cloak parted, exposing a belt of hair and human scalps. The pallid figure wore the armour of a warrior, with daggers strapped to calf and thigh, and another up his sleeve. A short sword and the Hammer of Og were thrust through his grisly belt. The eyes were slanted, and he had the elongated pupils of the elf, but his build was muscular like that of a man, betraying his mixed ancestry.

The eyes narrowed as he gazed at the Temple, his look one of cold calculation. A drifter, a mercenary and something of a renegade even within his craft, he was named Ares after the bastard son of the God Og and Brigitta – a minor godling in Og's multiple divinity. His name seemed prophetic, and his meagre elfin skills permitted him to outshine his counterparts in mock battles they held each day before the mercenary's guildhall to lure in potential customers. For he had an innate ability to anticipate any adversary's next move. A master of his craft, he was a shrewd businessman who always sold himself to the highest bidder, and his price was high indeed.

The pupils contracted to slits in the blaze of an invisible light. The unskilled eye would see nothing except the night fog that graced the island, but those with sight could see the dappled aura of magic power which surrounded the Wizards' College. It dazzled him.

The adventurer swung around slowly. The odd pupils dilated, growing large and round, compensating for the night. The warrior moved soundlessly away and the mist swallowed him, leaving not even a ripple in his wake.

Among his elfin skills was that of remaining obscure. He could move like a cat, and did. The warrior made his way down to the shoreline where he could view the port city of Abruzzi and rest his eyes from the radiant power that surrounded him.

The many white-robed clerics shifted restlessly in a tinkle of sweet chimes on either side of the chapel. Occasionally one would lean and whisper urgently to a neighbour. A white candle from their valuable hoard flickered in each hand, the many flames a symbol of the goddess spirit that united them. A hush fell as novice and initiate pondered the unprecedented ceremony. Every once in a while, there was a soft plop as wax dripped on to the floor.

The chapel doors opened, and the clerics swung round to regard the empty hall.

"Holy Brigitta, mother of all," the women intoned in unison.

The Matriarch, who was stationed below the statue of a Dove, turned with them, her voice joining the chant. Out of the corner of her eye, she noticed that many of the teachers and their assistants shot curious glances in her direction, wondering if their revered leader had lost her senses.

"Please accept another soul into your keeping," the assembled healers recited the sacred ritual of initiation.

A young woman appeared in the doorway, wearing a simple linen shift, and the high priestess of Brigitta had to admit that Zelia looked more natural in the unrestricted freedom of the flimsy sheath than she ever would in the formal robes of office.

Torchlight glinted off hair the colour of the deepest sapphire. Wild and unruly, it floated like a dark nimbus around her head. Her eyes were the frail shade of the winter sky, and in the bright light of day, one couldn't help but notice that her skin was a pale azure.

The chant swelled, "Invite her into your chapel."

The blue maid stepped through the doors.

"She has proven herself worthy . . ."

Around the Matriarch the many women and eunuchs who formed the teaching staff started a disgruntled muttering. Long ago, they had been scandalized at the half-breed's acceptance into this institution, but they could not refuse the generous donation the girl's father had sent with her, not to mention the additional endowment her stepmother had made from her own personal coffers.

"Skilled in craft, with healing hands and heart."

Few could deny that, her abilities were unsurpassed within the guild. The Matriarch let the words wash over her as her young protégée moved slowly down the central nave.

The women parted before their sister and closed in behind her, curling like an ocean current around an outcropping of rock. The maid looked nervously about her, skittish and ready to bolt, and the Matriarch felt a stab of pity.

The poor child had been shunted about since birth. The mother, an air elemental, had abandoned the suckling babe outside the father's tent. A lesser noble of Shamir, the father, one had to admit, had done the best he could for his troublesome daughter, placing her in the terem with the rest of the females and raising her as his own.

But the girl was more a thing of air than of earth, and she had been ill-suited for the submissive life of terem tents, where the desert tribes kept their womenfolk. She would constantly escape to disrupt her father's court. After thirteen turns, when Zelia came of age, the wayward child refused to take the veil, and within weeks she declined the auspicious match the twin sisters of fate, and her own recalcitrant nature, made for her.

Her lovely face had enchanted the Sultan of Shamir himself, and he had made an offer that no wise man would have rejected. Zelia's father had no choice but to accept, for it boiled down to the simplest terms: the sheik could welcome the Emir as a son-in-law and keep his head firmly planted between his shoulders, or find a suitable vessel or jar in which to keep it.

Her intended had been no less than the Emir of All Tribes; Light of Lights; The Manifestation of he who cannot be named – Ramman, the formless one and primary god of the Shamir; Holy of Holies; and, the Matriarch believed some 1,000 other names were attributed to the Sultan of Shamir. Her intended had also had some 400 wives, 2,000 concubines and 3,000 female slaves to do his bidding in his magnificently walled terem.

Unfortunately, Zelia was neither wise nor a man. When she heard of his proposal she spurned it with typical lack of tact and airy eloquence, saying that she'd sooner marry

Hades' imp than the Emir, whom she called a ton of quivering lard. It had not taken long for her words to make their way back to him.

Secretly, the Matriarch believed, the girl had done the right thing in refusing his favour; but only Zelia's immediate exile had saved her hapless father's life and the girl had been sent here to the healers' hall.

The Matriarch would have been only too happy to accept her without bribery, but Lady Hadidge, chief concubine to the sheik, had sweetened the father's gift with donations of her own to ensure the troublesome daughter stayed away. And who was the Matriarch to argue with largesse? Like any other girl-child, Zelia was a commodity to be bought and sold for a mere fraction of her actual worth. So she had exchanged the bangles and beads of the terem for the bells and heavy robes of the Healer.

The Matriarch sighed. She understood what it was like to be unwanted. Her own father had never quite forgiven her for not being the much-desired son. Then she had had the temerity to refuse to marry that fat, pompous windbag her own father had chosen for her. The break was complete when the Matriarch had joined the order. She wondered idly if her own father was alive or dead.

The priestess knew that the sheik missed his

eccentric child. Periodically, the father would send for Zelia, but after each summons, another generous donation would arrive from the Lady Hadidge's coffers so that there would be no embarrassing return of Zelia to her father's court.

". . . she comes to you in purity."

The women's chant penetrated her thoughts. The girl advanced slowly up the aisle, taking the prescribed step with each line that the sisters sang. As always, the Matriarch was struck by her diminutive size.

The young woman dropped to her knees before the Crown of Brigitta, and bent and kissed the hem of the holy mother's robe. Behind them, a voice hissed at the Matriarch.

"Last chance," it said, but the priestess shook her head in dismissal. The others didn't approve of Zelia's selection as second. Her tenure at the Healers' College was the longest on record. As a novice, she had mastered the notes and crystals easily enough. Only her herbcraft with its long hours of rote memorization and discipline presented a problem. Patient study did not number among her skills. Worse still, Zelia took to magic like a fire elemental to dry wood – an inborn gift from her fairy mother. The girl could no more deny the elemental side of her nature than a sand-snail could survive in the sea, and she craved the sorcerer's powers as her airy soul desired freedom and her parched throat thirsted for strong drink.

Her proclivities did not endear her to her instructors, and the girl was always being called to task for something. Each time Zelia had come close to achieving the next level, she got into some mischief and was held back. The Matriarch could do little about it. She could not show favouritism for any student, even her chosen, and when it came to scholastic advancement, the Matriarch's vote was just one of many on the board, carrying no more or less weight than the rest.

Only when it came to guild matters did the Matriarch's voice supersede her colleagues' clangour of contention. Thus, she had been able to intervene when Zelia was almost expelled for consorting with the sorcery students. As celibate sects, healers and wizards were kept apart and fraternizing was strictly forbidden. It was thought best to avoid temptation. With a certain amount of cynicism, the Matriarch pointed out that the guild would lose considerable income should the child leave their jurisdiction, and then vetoed expulsion as imprudent. The board had been forced to turn a blind eye to Zelia's male cohorts.

Privately, the priestess noted that the child

did not lose her abilities as a result of this association, as was predicted by wizardly legend and myth. So another convention was shattered in the woman's mind. To the Matriarch, Zelia was a breath of fresh air that wafted away the fusty atmosphere of tradition. She was perfect for the task the Matriarch had set for her – to storm the all-male bastion of wizardry and shake its citadel, the college, down to its foundations.

Zelia shifted, as if she caught the undercurrent of her mistress's musings, and blushed. The Matriarch nodded her approval. The girl's behaviour had been impeccable for the past few months – although the priestess had had to keep the child busy – and finally the governing board could no longer refuse her initiation. The Matriarch had let slip to the appropriate source – Fidhl was always good for carrying a tale – that the sheik's endowment would increase as soon as the girl achieved full status and this had permitted her to hasten the ceremony. The Matriarch fervently hoped that the blessed Brigitta would forgive her that one small lie.

From there, it had been only one small step to name her as successor, and no one could gainsay that choice. The child would never know what her mistress had gone through to see this moment.

The high priestess stared down at the swirling cloud of blue hair and winced an unseen apology at the top of the woman's bowed head. *Forgive me, my child*, the Matriarch thought, and she wondered if she was doing the right thing, installing Zelia before the council had truly accepted her.

"Rise," the Matriarch said, taking the woman by the hand and lifting her up. Then she turned to her peers, the Grand Council of Healers. The reverend mother extended both arms.

The Mistress of Crystals hurried up with the robes, pausing briefly to whisper in the Matriarch's ear, "Illustrious mother, are you sure?"

The priestess scowled and Zelia turned questioning eyes from one cleric to the other.

The Matriarch placed the radiant robes on the slender blue shoulders. The robes shimmered with stunning brilliance in the collective glow of the candles. Slivers of pure quartz crystal were woven into the warp, and shards of amethyst into the woof. Depending on the light, the initiate's robes could be all colours or no colours at all, so the initiate appeared more luminscent than the novice, who wore plain white linen. Some said that even to look upon the cloth was healing, but the Matriarch knew better. It was simply a device to aid concentration and help both patient and healer fall into the healing trance.

The Matriarch's hands tingled where they rested lightly on the girl's shoulders. The crystal in the cloth vibrated to the initiate's spirit, and the High Priestess set aside all doubts. She was sure her decision was the right one. The future lay with this child.

The Matriarch embraced her protégée and muttered a couple of words of encouragement, before repeating the accepted liturgy.

"We take you unto the bosom of Brigitta, Zelia Al Y Kazzam. You are one of us, accepted into the sisterhood. Where once you shone with the single light of the crystal, now you burn with the candle's flame, one of the many lights of Brigitta. Do you swear to administer to the sick and wounded according to her precepts, never taking a human life?"

"I do," the young maid answered.

The Matriarch swung slowly back to the council and gestured for the Mistress of the Bells to step forward. Each of the finely wrought chimes rang on a single liquid note, and each note had the power to heal. The healer must learn them all, and every one of the bells must be earned. Only when the note and its healing properties were mastered did the novice receive the robes of an initiate.

According to tradition, the novice must come as clean as a babe to the house of Brigitta for her resurrection and redemption into the sisterhood, and so the bells were taken away during ritual cleansing the night before and returned only after the robes had been received and the initiate forsworn.

The Matriarch passed the chimes one after another to Zelia. As each tolled, the women hummed the corresponding note so that they rang out across the chapel in a floating, lilting harmony. The Mistress of the Bells faltered before handing the last bell to the Matriarch to give her superior one final imploring look. The Matriarch retrieved the bell from the woman's hands and excused her without so much as a nod.

Then the Crown of Brigitta drew the bell from around her own neck, and instead of humming the pure, clear C upon which it rang, the assemblage gasped as one. Even the maiden's eyes widened. The high priestess stared defiantly back at her audience.

No one but the Matriarch recognized Zelia's unique gift and nurtured it. Few were born with magical talent, and fewer still could master it. Women were denied it. If what the Matriarch had seen in Brigitta's pool was true, the healers needed Zelia's skill now more than ever.

The priestess would *not* have dissent at this late date.

The Matriarch looped the leather thong over Zelia's neck, and turned to present her to the congregation as chosen second and heir. The group was supposed to respond with some sign of recognition. The silence echoed harshly throughout the hall.

Usually, the new acolyte was swiftly surrounded as friends rushed forward to give their congratulations, but none swooped down to praise or applaud Zelia. The crowd hung back nervously. The maiden fidgeted, her fingers twitching at the crystalline cloth. One by one, the instructors scuttled forth to mutter words of reserved praise, and the Matriarch was pained to see how difficult pretty speech came from those who one day must accept the girl's orders as they accepted her own.

With saddened eyes, the Matriarch watched Zelia leave. The girl's joy was such that she seemed impervious to the slight that had been done her. Besides, Zelia had her other "friends" with whom she could celebrate with true airy abandon. The Matriarch shook her head in sorrow.

The die was cast. The girl's natural inclinations would do the rest.

* * *

Raucous voices surrounded the cloaked form of the stranger. The many students ignored his lurking presence, having no reason to fear him. The young wizards were on their turf and, cloaked and clad as he was, the adventurer's weapons were not visible.

He had no wish to be noticed. He had come here to find warmth away from the damp chill of the Thessalian night. From the depths of his hood, Ares' gaze swept the room. The noisy exuberance of the crowd was made all the more loud and jarring by the iridescent magic which radiated from the inn's clientele in waves so bright they hurt his eyes.

His eye lit on one customer in particular and lingered there. Her robes proclaimed her a healer, but magic shone from her like a beacon. Ares wondered if the others were blind to her talent. It bleached and diminished that of the other students, until they appeared as mere sparks against a candle's steady flame, or a flame against the sun.

Perhaps their lack of concern had another source, for they dealt with her as a friend and a comrade. Even now one student in the robes of an advanced journeyman had his arm draped casually around the slender shoulders. Perhaps they guarded her secret, for surely such a woman would make great fuel for the witch's pyre.

A pointed ear pricked as he listened to brief snatches of conversation. Odd bits of spells and incantations, lively debates over the proper gestures and genuflections – they came to him in pieces and he could make no sense of them.

The half-elf reached up and pulled his cloak further down to hide his features before sinking deeper into the shadows of the pub. He did not want his face or his craft to be recognized. Elves were the near-human descendants of elementals so transformed that they had become every bit as mortal as man. A part of the magic that was left behind when the portals closed, they were not welcomed by the wizards who guarded their craft well.

For the most part, though, elves lived peaceably alongside man. They stayed in separate enclaves, wrapped in deep mystifying mists to prevent man's entrance into their domain. The sea elves had built a great city in Shalop along the western coast. The wood elves frequented the forests in the foothills of the great mountain chain that formed the continent's spine. Ares' own kin, the snow elves, carved their castles from solid ice in the far northern tip of Szatmar.

Had he been pure-blood elf, Ares need not have worried. Students such as these would have dealt with him as a curiosity. Most would have tried to glean elfin magic from him. However, few could help but notice his human qualities, and half-breeds were generally viewed with suspicion by both races. The elves would not accept them because they believed their blood to be tainted, the mist put in place as much to keep the impure out as the human. And the human envied them their reputed magical talents and their extended lifespan.

This close to the college was no place for one of his kind. Ares normally avoided coming this far south. His land was to the north, beyond the city-states of Ticino, in Uri and beyond. His home was Og's home, the northern lands of the continent of Eubonia. In the countries of Szatmar and Norvon, none could surpass his skill, and war was always ripe for the making.

It had always been his home. As a child he had been found outside the stone circle of Szatmar. The circle's magic was so powerful that nothing grew for many leagues around it, and Ares often wondered if its magic had somehow stripped him of his memories, for he recalled nothing of his early childhood. Few strayed there but the mad, and the man who had found Ares had been as crazy as they come – a follower of the iron-god Og, patron to all berserkers and, vicariously, adventurers and mercenaries.

Og's cult encouraged conversion at knife-point. His "father" had been an ardent believer. A man of little patience, he didn't ask questions but simply slit the throat of any unbeliever. The church hierarchy had decided his method a little precipitous since it didn't permit the potential convert the chance to consider his options.

His master, Wulf, had been excommunicated and he had then dedicated his life to the extermination of all unbelievers. From this unlikely benefactor, Ares got his name, his weapons and his calling.

Og's worshippers could be found anywhere mercenaries are used, even in the southern continent of Daklha. And Ares was good, very good. Many of his peers had moved south where the competition from him wasn't so stiff. Like any adventurer, Ares had more than his share of enemies and envious friends. There was no telling what would happen if any one of his "old friends" discovered his presence. Many would have quite happily accused him of illegal sorcery, for Ares seemed to have an unfair advantage in any battle, always knowing his foe's next move before he made it.

Despite the danger, the mercenary had been drawn here like a puppet on a string. He sensed a great magic in the making – a sorcery working beyond the normal fields and grids of masters.

It had called to him, pulling at him, just as the blue halo that wreathed the healer now drew his eye from across the room.

A young journeyman magician produced a small image of a Quattarean slave girl. It danced in shimmering elegance on his palm. Ares' mouth dropped open, and he felt a rush of envy at the young wizard's talent.

The wanderer's magical skills were few. From his elfin forebears, Ares was blessed with night sight and could slither through shadows with the stealth of a werecat. He could recognize true wizardry when it happened, and he could watch a spell on the wing, searching for its intended target. When the five moons were in the right position, the adventurer could view the glittering, sinewy cords of the ley line, the magical grid that connected the stone circles of power and from which, it was said, all sorcery came. But he could not manipulate it or command it to his use.

Ares leaned forward, fascinated by the exquisitely crafted shade. He was something of an illusionist who relied upon sleight of hand. This did nothing to redeem him among his peers but he didn't care. He had been a mercenary for too many years to care about men's good opinions. The only thing Ares valued was their fear.

The healer shouted at the youth and slapped

at the undulating dancer. The porcelain figure shattered, and the healer growled something incomprehensible to the twittering group before retreating to the bar to stand next to a Quattarean slaver.

The slaver's gaze raked the crowd, coming to rest on Ares. Underneath his cloak, Ares' body stiffened. The Quattarean jostled the healer's elbow, and she swore at him vehemently. The slave trader turned his attention back to the small girl. The warrior's tense shoulder relaxed, and he sunk back into his corner.

The healer jabbed at the slaver's arm. The many golden rings, which were the Quattarean's trademark, clattered harshly.

"Vermin!" her voice rose among the crowd. The man's reply was slurred as much by the rings that pierced his lips as with drink. He teetered tipsily, leering most unpleasantly at her. The blue maid didn't recoil or back away, instead she seemed to lean towards the slaver, as if she wanted to incite his wrath.

A fight was brewing. Conversation ceased as the students chose sides. Ares' hand strayed to the dagger at his calf, and the mercenary cursed himself again for coming here. He was crazy to have come so far from his home base. There he was close to his kith and kin, the snow elves, even if he had been never able to penetrate the mists that surrounded their domain. He would leave on the morrow, taking the dawn ferry for the mainland, and forget this foolish idea of chasing after magic.

The slave trader shoved the girl roughly. She staggered slightly, steadied herself and held her ground. Quietly, Ares drew his knife and at the same moment, the healer's robes parted to reveal a particularly nasty-looking Shamirian scimitar.

The world around him exploded. Fireballs flew to and fro. An apprentice squealed like a pig, only an instant before he became one, and Ares ducked out of the door. This wasn't his kind of fight.

Thessalia, on Pelopnos the Isle of Learning, was the home of both Wizards' and Healers' Colleges. With so many spells flying about it wasn't surprising for a street to appear or disappear suddenly. Usually no permanent damage was done. The Cock and Boar wavered ponderously upon occasion but, a favourite among sorcery students – and much tenanted by them in their dark robes emblazoned with the symbols of the planets, gods and moons – the public house rarely vanished.

In the white robes of her craft, Zelia Al Y Kazzam was an oddity. Most healers had neither time nor temperament for revelry or debate, and it was thought unseemly for a woman to go out alone after dark. Her appearance, if not her rough, rude manner, presented a striking contrast to the other customers. Her skin was a soft dusky blue, inherited from her wrong-side-of-the-blanket air elemental mother, and her hair, the colour of indigo night, matched the dark robes of the mages.

She was a regular customer, and the barman Thesbos had grown used to her strange ways and didn't pay much attention when her *kymus*-thickened voice rose above the rest. Nor did he take any heed when she drew her blade – a wicked Shamirian scimitar – on the Quattarean slaver.

The trader's response was quick. He yanked her around, holding a knife to her throat. His dagger began to glow and his sleeve burst into flame, and then Thesbos *was* surprised.

Such wizardry wasn't permitted any female, healer or not!

Things were getting out of hand, the barman decided, as he dodged a fireball released by a journeyman wizard in defence of the woman who so obviously needed no defending. Thesbos bounded over the counter, and the slaver fell into the healer's arms with Zelia's blade planted in his breast, his charred arm still aflame.

Thesbos darted behind a fallen table just as a clumsy apprentice turned himself and his nearest neighbours into a pile of squirming centipedes in a spell thrown wild, so that it bounced off the walls and rebounded on its creator. Another student squealed like a pig. His nose flattened to form a snout. His arms and legs shrank. His fingers retracted into his hands to become hooves. The young initiate's wriggling, pink body tangled in his robes as he tried to struggle free.

By then Thesbos had forgotten all about the woman who had powers she shouldn't have, or about the College Guard which would surely arrive soon. A table next to him sprouted wings and flew off, and after that, he needed all his wits to keep himself alive, intact, and in his natural shape until the following morning.

The adventurer hunched low against the cutting wind. Lightning, invisible to human eye, snaked from the windows of the pub. A brilliant flash was followed quickly by flares of red, yellow, green, orange, purple – so many colours that the fog turned a muddy brown.

Another more material glare joined that of the interwoven spells, orange-red, gold and flickering. Fire! The tavern was awash with flame and Ares hesitated, wondering whether or not he should return and rescue the maiden, when she emerged coughing and choking from the pyre, dragging the slaver behind her. The healer lowered his body to the ground and considered him for a moment before she knelt and placed her hands on the gaping wound. A brilliant glow engulfed both healer and patient. Ares felt bones knit, muscles twine and blood vessels join under her touch. The wound closed and the scar faded to a thin white line. The charred skin dried and flaked away, leaving flesh as tender and pink as a baby's. Ares was amazed. This went beyond anything known to healer-craft or wizardry. This was high sorcery!

The woman sat back. After a moment's meditation, she touched the man's forehead, muttering a forgetfulness spell. The halo dimmed. Her shoulders drooped and he could feel her fatigue. She stood, rubbing her face with her hands, before staggering off into the night.

The slaver jerked upright and scrambled to his feet. His eyes lit upon the burning inn and then he too turned and fled. Ares, watching in his dark corner, decided things were just starting to get interesting. Perhaps he'd hang around for a few more days. . . .

Thud! Thud! THUD!

Zelia, daughter of Sheik Al Yabbah Y Kazzam, was awakened by a rhythmic thumping that thrust splinters of glass into her brain. Her pulse pounded past her temples, as if one of her father's fine Shamirian stallions was stampeding inside her skull, and the young woman opened a single bleary eye to a cruelly bright day and groaned.

She pulled a pillow over her head.

Thud! Thud! THUD!

Only then did Zelia realize that at least some of the banging came from the door. She sat up and immediately regretted it. Her stomach lurched into her throat, and her head followed its own swirling course around the room.

"Yes," she croaked. "Who is it?"

A voice, muffled by the thick wooden door, uttered a fuzzy response.

"Wait a moment." She groped blindly, snatching her student's gown from a jumbled pile of dirty clothes. Holding it up, she saw that it was stained, yellow and red. She plunged head and arms through it without thinking.

The door opened and Zelia recognized the Matriarch's pasty-faced assistant, Fidhl. His eyes took in at a glance the stacks of unwashed dishes, the mouldy bread crusts and the shrivelled melon rinds before they fell on the scrolls – scrolls of forbidden sorcery, ancient maps of the magical ley, and pieces of proscribed spells. Bits of parchment covered with odd runes were tucked between talismans and strange relics and scattered among even stranger metal gadgets. Items of sinful sorcery were stuffed in corners and piled precariously on shelves – things Zelia had received as gifts or "borrowed" from her boyfriends through the years. Fidhl cleared his throat and, averting his gaze from the heretical collection, turned again to face her directly.

"You have been summoned," he said.

Zelia nodded her acknowledgement. "I will

join you in a moment. I must change." She plucked at the stained robe.

"Now!" he said, sniffing his disdain.

With the discipline of long practice, Zelia recited a relaxation mantra and took a couple of deep gulps of air, in a ritual *pranayama*. Her head stopped spinning at each slight motion.

"Would you have me go like this?" She shrugged and the bleeding-heart splashed across her chest fluttered.

He eyed her and acquiesced.

"Get out and let me dress in peace." Zelia threw her head back defiantly, which immediately set the room whirling about her again. She coughed weakly to hide her momentary discomfort and the acolyte backed out of the room. She tore through the clothes she had discarded in a tangled knot on her bench, looking for something clean to wear. Nothing! As she slipped from the soiled robe, she spied the formal gown of her office glittering on a hook in the corner of the room. The maid seized her initiate's robes and tugged them over her head and shoulders, her body protesting against each movement.

Zelia winced, tried to remember what had happened the night before and drew a blank. The summons from the administratrix of the Healers' College was not unusual, nor even unexpected, but Fidhl's attitude was mildly disturbing. Perhaps she had celebrated a touch more than was prudent last night.

Strong drink will be the death of me yet, she thought as she stood in front of the mirror to ponder her reflection. Her colouring was wrong, more green than blue, and her eyes were red and rheumy. She drew trembling fingers through her thick mane and spun one last time before the mirror, instantly regretting it. Resting against the doorframe, she groaned.

Much subdued, Zelia went to join the eunuch in the dark hall. He shambled before her with a loose-limbed gait, making for the street. Just before the door he halted and waited for her to catch up.

Sunlight blazed across the broad boulevard, and Zelia stifled a gasp as her head began to pulse again. They moved outside and the fresh air nearly made her swoon. He urged her forward. The broad avenue along which they walked divided the healers' quarters from the wizards' residences.

The two groups didn't intermingle, but in this, as in many other things, Zelia was the exception. The young initiate smiled as they passed a spot where she had once had a rendezvous or tryst with a lover. Zelia remembered few names. As soon as she learned what magic she could from one student, she moved on to the next, who was inevitably of a higher grade and more advanced degree. But she remembered each and every spell. She had written them down religiously, squirrelling the scraps among her things.

Occasionally, stray wisps of magic would escape from the dorms and the student halls to colour the street red, blue, purple or green. The two acolytes moved untouched, surrounded by a cacophony of sound. The townspeople scrambled to get out of their way. Today the tinkling of chimes that adorned ankle and wrist evoked pain in Zelia's already throbbing skull, and she silenced the bells with a whispered spell. The eunuch's back stiffened at this blatant use of illicit power.

A cloud passed over the sun, and Zelia shivered with a sudden premonition. The two acolytes entered the college's cool interior, its walls white marble inlaid with mother-of-pearl. Two of the castrata joined them in the outer enclave, bringing up the rear. Zelia regarded them suspiciously and grimaced. Pulling her shoulders back, she flowed through the inner sanctum led by the scurrying cleric. Usually the tranquillity of the place soothed her turbulent spirit, but today it left her unmoved.

The assistant stopped before a crystal door.

Zelia drew a deep breath and nodded, stepping into the college's crystalline heart. The cleric followed while the two castrata stationed themselves at the door, positioned in such a way as to prevent escape. *Not a good sign*.

The inner gardens were resplendent. The sweet scent of herbs permeated the air. The glaring sun was muted, reflected and refracted off the carved walls and roof until it spilled rainbows of laughing liquid light. For Zelia, the healer's glory was exquisite torture. The prismatic illumination cut through her cornea, slicing into her brain like a hot knife. She shrivelled from the unrelenting cheeriness, and the dark blade of ill omen twisted in her stomach.

With a show of confidence she did not feel, Zelia raised her eyes to face her mentor where she sat perched on the ledge next to Brigitta's holy pool. The Matriarch did not turn from the healing waters that could cure any number of mortal ills, neither did she make any move to acknowledge her protégée's presence. Zelia coughed gently into her hand, and her mistress swung to confront her most gifted and most irksome student, her face grim.

The Matriarch rose with a strident clatter of bells, one arm outstretched, her fingers curled tight, forming a clenched fist. Opening her hand she revealed Zelia's chosen crystal, the stone from her native Shamir, the one that she had been required to bring with her in order to gain entrance into Brigitta's House. According to ancient tradition, it contained her soul and through its manipulations the teachers could control the students, and initiate the novice.

Zelia's pupils rounded with shock, and she shrank away from her mistress.

"You have desecrated your craft. You have done the unforgivable in the taking of a human life. Shame and anathema be upon you!" The Matriarch seemed to grow as she spoke the ritual words of excommunication. "I will recommend that in ten days hence you be tried. If found guilty, we will drive you from this temple and expel you from our sacred order. May Brigitta turn her face from you. May the gift of healing dry up in your veins, turning your blood to dust. In ten days hence, the tribunal will meet, Zelia Al Y Kazzam, and we shall decide whether or not you are to be permanently damned as one of the fallen. If we find you such, may your name be cursed and your punishment posted in every market, every town and every city so that you may never practice your craft again."

The woman's arm moved in a slow arc towards the rainbow-studded ceiling. She threw the stone against the floor. It shattered, and the younger woman collapsed at the Matriarch's feet.

Some time later, Zelia sat alone in her room, hugging her knees to her chest. Banned from her craft? How could this be? The Matriarch said she had killed a man, but Zelia couldn't remember a thing. Still, if the Matriarch said she had killed, then she had killed. The Matriarch would not lie.

What could Zelia do now? Where could she go? She considered briefly returning to her father's tent and quailed at the thought. At least here she could show her face. She could no more take the veil than a fish could fly, and she doubted if she would be welcomed by her father's chief wife and concubine. Her father would embrace her quickly enough. He loved her well and tolerated her peculiarities – for perhaps he had some small memory of Zelia's mother – but the Lady Hadidge would not appreciate the girl's return.

Zelia fingered the message that had come to her earlier that day. Marked with the Matriarch's seal, it was her only hope. The young initiate, who was an initiate no more, placed her head on her knees and wept.

* * *

Night fell. The third moon rose as Zelia stole into the crystal citadel of Brigitta to attend the Matriarch's summons. She paused just inside the crystal door. It took a few minutes for her eyes to adjust from dark to light. There was a soft rustle of movement. Zelia started as the Matriarch stepped from behind a flowing curtain of flowers. Her heart thundered in her chest.

"My child, thank you for meeting me."

"I should not be here, Mistress. If you were caught with me . . ." She finished the sentence with a shudder.

"I would still be Matriarch, as you will be in your time."

"But . . ."

"Hush." The priestess placed a finger to her lips. "These are strange times we live in, Zelia, but we do not have time to discuss them now."

The older woman grasped the young maiden's hand and led her urgently to the pool. "I have something you must see."

Knowing her mistress as she did, Zelia did not question her further, only knelt as instructed and peered into the glassy surface. The rainbow lights danced and swirled across it until a picture began to form on the darkened waters.

Zelia inhaled sharply. "Who—?"

The Matriarch waved her hand over the water and the image dissolved. "That was Queb."

"Queb, the necromancer? But surely he's—"

"Dead." The Matriarch finished the sentence for her. "I suspect not."

"Why? I mean, how can you be sure he lives?"

"Because the pool revealed something else which had not yet occurred, at least not then." The Matriarch studied her hands as though something in them interested her greatly.

The braceleted hand darted out and touched the water, and an image of the old Cock and Boar surfaced. "And this, does this look familiar to you?"

Zelia recognized herself and watched in horror as the Quattarean slave trader folded into her arms.

"Holy mother!" Zelia gestured expansively. "I don't know *what* happened. I don't remember a thing."

"It was meant to be, or else I would not have seen it here," the Matriarch said.

"But a human life?"

"A slaver." The Matriarch grimaced. Her face reflected off the many crystals in her headdress in a thousand little frowns.

"I thought it was only the Shamirian that despised the Quattareans," Zelia commented.

"No, it is not only the traders in horseflesh

who hate those that deal in human flesh. No, I prefer to think of all the people who will live their turns in freedom because of your act."

Zelia said nothing.

"Don't you see? You were sacrificed to Brigitta."

The maid blinked in surprise. The Matriarch caught her baffled look and said, "I could have stopped you, prevented your folly, but I didn't. I saw this. I *knew* what you were going to do before it happened."

"I don't understand."

"Brigitta's mirror doesn't only reflect things past. More often it shows things that have yet to be. But always, *always* what it reveals will affect the sisterhood in some way. Thus Queb's appearance must be a warning from Brigitta. And if not a warning, then who but Queb could bend Brigitta's pool to his will, and what could he possibly be seeking that would lie here?"

Zelia lifted her shoulders in a shrug.

"Could it be," the Matriarch continued as if she hadn't noticed, "that he seeks a wild talent, an as-yet untried talent as powerful as his own?"

The young woman looked incredulous. "What about the wizards? Surely one among their number would be of more interest to him, and if this is one of their number, shouldn't they be told?"

"That bunch of cackling old hens couldn't produce a broken egg between them, much less talent! They would stifle it immediately," the Matriarch snorted. "Besides, I did talk to that old toad Malevolent," she said, using her personal nickname for the Archmage. "And he would not listen. He's as inflexible as an earth elemental. He does not believe me. He wants proof. That is where you come in. I want you to bring back that proof. Proof that Queb exists. His staff would radiate to his vibrations, would it not?"

"Well, yes, it should," Zelia said.

"Then that should do. Can you bring back his staff?"

"He won't give it up willingly."

"That is why I must send you. It would appear that this burden is yours alone to bear. Who else among us has your . . . skills?"

"Skills? I dabble. Surely you can think of someone better than myself for this. A delegation, perhaps?"

The Matriarch gave the water a little stir. A green field with a sparkling fountain appeared. Zelia stared fearfully into the pond.

"How much do you know of Queb and his destruction?" the Matriarch said.

"My scrolls tell me little, and most of it is cryptic. I know that his powers were such that he was able to do what no other mortal could do. He pierced the nine planes and consorted with the denizens of the Death's Realm, the planes of Night and Hades. It took all the wizards at the college, and in the courts spread across the many lands, to defeat the Archmage in a battle that destroyed the wizards' old college . . ."

The Matriarch interrupted, finishing for her pupil, a note of bitterness in her voice, ". . . creating in the Great Northern Wastes an area so inhospitable that they had to quit the place and move the college to Pelopnos, taking over Brigitta's temple and expelling the healers to another lesser building. Which, I suppose, was to our advantage and our gain." The Matriarch grinned. "For we found the pool of Brigitta."

The high priestess motioned impatiently. "But all that is common knowledge. Do you know what became of Queb? What they did to him?"

The girl frowned. "Imprisoned him between planes, I believe."

"Have you ever asked yourself how? No mortal man, even Queb, has ever been able to enter the circle of stones or travel between the planes and survive. No mortal, except . . ." She gave her protégée a sidelong glance.

Zelia gasped. "My father? But how does that link me to Queb?"

The holy mother pointed at the pond and the green circle beyond. "The place is not of this plane. See the flowers there? They are not found anywhere on this world that I know of. And what healer, except perchance the Mistress of Lore, knows herbcraft better than I?"

The maid simply stared at her, mouth agape.

"The wizards did not have the skill so they asked for and got help from the elementals. 'Twas your fairy relations who sprang the trap. Then one of their number was set to guard the door – one so flighty, so capricious, that she could not be persuaded by any of his promises fair or foul."

"Who?"

"Who do you think?" the Matriarch said as she indicated the pool. There was a disturbance in the air over the fountain. It seemed to flit around the circle, darting to and fro. Occasionally, Zelia caught a glimpse of hand, foot, leg or wing, and if she turned her head so that she wasn't looking directly at the creature, a figure emerged of a tiny female clad in gossamer and whimsy.

"My mother?" Zelia breathed softly.

"I suspect so." The Matriarch felt Zelia's turmoil as she regarded the tiny fairy.

"Why did she abandon me?" the girl said forlornly.

"She could do none other, child. You are mortal like your sire, made of solid flesh, blood and sinew. You have mortal mass, small as you are. Your mother could fit in the palm of your hand. She can expand, like smoke can expand, but only by becoming so distended that she would soon dissipate. I suppose if she grew large enough she would simply cease to exist. So you see, your mother could not have fed you or cared for you. The victuals of such flimsy beings would not have nourished a mortal child. Only by taking you to your human sire could you have survived. Do not think too unkindly of her, Zelia – she loves you. Of this, I am sure. Sometimes, through the years, I have seen her face in the pool. I believe she watches over you still.

"Look at her for a minute," the priestess said. "See how she flutters from one end of the glade to another, as if she were searching for something. Could it be that Queb, whom she was set to guard, has escaped?"

"But . . ." The picture of fountain and fairy vanished, returning to show Zelia as she dragged the slaver's corpse from the burning tavern.

"I believe this was necessary," the Matriarch gestured at the frozen scene. "Although I've oft wondered why the scene stopped there and I saw nothing else. But the ways of the goddess are mysterious and cannot be questioned. It seems you *must* be permitted to leave the temple and travel abroad. To combat this evil you will need to be free from the rules of temple and guild. You see, there," the Matriarch nodded at the Zelia in the crystalline pool, "the bell of office, don't you? This is the vision as it appeared to me before the event. Your wearing the bell could only mean that you had already received your robes and been pronounced as successor. I arranged the ceremony after I saw this the first time, overriding all objections, knowing full well you would do what you have done. So in the final analysis, I suppose you could say I set you up."

"And I am named renegade, my stone shattered and my craft denied me."

"Not your stone." The high priestess withdrew the Shamirian crystal from her robes. "Nor your craft. None can take your skill from you."

The Matriarch passed the stone to Zelia and it pulsed with the beating of her heart.

"The other was a fake. The crystals of Shamir are much loved and not all that difficult to come by in the port city of Abruzzi," the woman explained. "The ritual was a sham. It will appease your detractors until the formal hearing ten days from now. I hope to prevent your actual expulsion from the guild. You have a tenday to prepare yourself. Ten days to flee. You will be protected from civil authorities by the guild until then, and I will do all in my power to delay the proceedings. Beyond that time, the healers cannot help you. Indeed, if I am right about Queb, we could be destroyed if we tried to protect you."

Zelia shook her head, with a shimmer of sapphire blue, bewildered at all the woman had told her.

The priestess dipped her hand into the water, cupped it and poured it over the image of bloodstained healer. Little waves rippled outward, and the picture was disturbed, blurred by the ever-widening circles.

"Even if the rest of the craft turns against you, you will remain my second. For the Crown of Brigitta's right to choose her heir is sacrosanct, and none can gainsay her choosing. I can stay the hand of the guild, but the civil authorities will pursue you. Murder is still a crime. Thus, I recommend that you make your preparations quickly and be far from Pelopnos' shores before the tenday is up."

The girl looked gloomily at her feet.

"Tut, child, you have always craved freedom, and you shall not be alone. There's one other you can trust," the Matriarch said.

"Only one?" Zelia asked.

"Only one," the priestess said and tried to make her smile a reassuring one.

Again the necromancer was taken by surprise as a young woman appeared, hazy and vague, to float in the middle of his laboratory. The wizard quivered with rage as he recognized his ancient adversary – the indigo hair, the delicate blue skin, and the cerulean eyes. Those eyes linked with his and their colour changed to steely grey, the cast of storm clouds. His enemy made flesh.

Queb's fingers tightened and the herbs he held in his hand were crushed, bleeding green. He spun in a swirl of black robes and zapped the faceless homunculus who waited patiently to do his bidding. The featureless form exploded.

The wizard massaged his hands, manipulating each knobbly arthritic finger, and then turned back to the hovering spectre in blue. He had found her at last!

CHAPTER 4

The dead walked!

Zelia's jaw unhinged, and she gawped, for there was the slaver braying his wares – six-legged dung-camels! *Used* dung-camels! The Quattarean was easily recognizable, for he exhibited the square and protruding jaw of all his people, and his ears, nose and mouth were studded with many rings.

"Fine dung-camels!" he bellowed as Zelia dashed through the crowded marketplace and the crowds hastened to get out of her way.

"Dung-camels! Good sturdy beasts!"

A path opened before her through the crush of human bodies – few dared cross the path of the witch who had destroyed the Cock and Boar. Her temper was getting shorter by the minute and their fawning behaviour was starting to annoy her. Zelia elbowed her way through the throng until she reached the spectre.

As she approached, he turned to her. "Ah, young lady, here to see my stock?" He didn't seem to know her. "You have a fine Shamirian scimitar, I see."

Zelia flinched. The man was complimenting her on her blade – the same blade that had penetrated his breast less than two days ago.

"Then you are a person of the desert and one who can truly appreciate the virtues of these beasts. One of Ramman's most blessed creatures," he said, mentioning the primary god of Shamir rather than the cruel Quattarean god, Apsu the Devourer. "A remarkable beast of burden. Its muck can heat a house for years, as long as it lives, and after its death, the meat is tasty and the hide makes sturdy leather. Take this animal here," and he patted its rump and reached under the beast to stroke each of its eight stomachs in turn. "This animal was owned by a little lady in Hamadan, the country of culture and education in the southern desert. Its dung burned only once a tenday, during religious celebrations, I believe."

Out of the corner of her eye, Zelia saw a glimmer of silver-white hair such as one would expect to find on a venerated oldster, but these braids surrounded the fierce face of a warrior. It was not the first time that she had noted the vague presence, but whenever she turned, whoever it was had gone.

The renegade healer silenced the trader with a cutting motion, her hand slicing the air. "Don't you know me?"

"My lady, with a face like that, such a picture of loveliness – how could I forget such a one as you?" he replied.

This man was good, Zelia thought. *He'd do well in his new profession.*

"I met you two nights ago," she said.

"Ah," he said knowingly. "That night's a bit vague. The only thing I remember was waking up in the street outside the Cock and Boar, covered in blood. It was an inferno." And Zelia nodded her head in agreement, for she had gone to view the devastation earlier that day. All that remained of her one-time haunt on the squalid side street near the docks was a charred skeleton that looked like a beached sea-dragon stripped of its meat.

"Wizards were battling all about me, and as you probably know, it is not wise to stay where there's magic flying about. I lost my memory, I did." He tugged an earring. "Can't for the life of me remember who I am. Probably got hit by some spell. I suppose it will come back to me, though, and I've got this fine job so I'll be all right. You sure I can't interest you in a camel?"

Zelia shook her head no and left to wander the market square, bemused. Her victim was living and well, healed most likely by herself. It seemed her healer's abhorrence of death dominated even her innate hatred of the Quattarean. She had sensed the subtle workings of magic. A forgetfulness spell perhaps? Or maybe he had reformed? The maid smirked contemptuously. Her grin widened when the trader turned to tout the virtues of the same broken-down camel, exclaiming this time that it had only been driven to temples by a little old lady from Al Khali.

Reformed indeed!

She shrugged. Now that she knew the slaver was alive and she no betrayer of her craft, the burden of guilt was lifted from her shoulders. She relaxed visibly. Her stride lengthened as she moved more confidently through the crowd, deciding that she quite liked her newfound freedom and her rôle as renegade. Her fabled skills suited her purpose nicely, an easy escape, and the reputed murder suited her guild. Both kept people out of her way and ensured their compliance. Most were eager to accept any offer, no matter how ludicrous, if only to get her out of their establishment before the place was caught in inferno's fire or a plague of demons descended from Hades' realm to devour their stores.

The stationer held his fingers crossed to ward off the evil eye the entire time she was present, and the tailor bowed and scraped, agreeing with her every word.

"Leather leggings to fit you? Yes, mum," he said without batting an eyelash at the unusual request. "And a jerkin. Ticinian leather? Very good choice, mum. What about the style? I could show you some pictures of the very latest in fashion." He pulled some placards from behind his counter and fanned them out before her. She studied them, thought of the shimmer of white among the crowd and picked one. The tailor bent to read the print. "*Moderate Mercenary*. Quite popular this year, I must say."

Zelia handed him her crystal robes of office and gave him instructions, redesigning them for her less-than-subdued tastes.

"Cut it off here," she said, indicating a length far above the knee, and a slit up the sides." She turned sideways and pointed from her armpit to her waist. "From here to here," she indicated an area from her waist to her thigh. What remained was little more than a tunic that would show plenty of shapely calf, and allow a tantalizing glimpse of thigh and flank.

He opened his mouth to question her, took one look at the indigo hair and blue skin, and thought better of it.

"And make a belt from the scraps," she added as an afterthought, "to hold it closed."

"Ah," he said with sudden insight. "The clean sweeping lines of the classic Gekko period."

"Huh?" she said.

"And when would you be wanting all this?"

Zelia tilted her head to one side and considered for a minute. "Tomorrow."

"Of course," he said, seemingly unconcerned, but as she left, Zelia noticed him brandish the Bear Claw of Urrl about the room to exorcise her presence. The healer chuckled, her humour very much restored. She'd wager that the clothes would be well made. Obviously the tailor feared her sorcery more than the desecration of her healer's robes.

Ares backed into a dusky corner when the blue maid arrived at the stable. On these back streets it wasn't easy blending into the crowd. The stablemaster approached the woman cautiously. A cruel, ham-fisted man, with a twisted, broken nose, he had been less than pliant during their previous meeting, dickering over price. All he had been willing to offer her then was equal trade, horse for horse. The poor mare could not compare with her noble Shamirian stallion. One look at its half-starved appearance, and the woman's temper had flared, rising like a tempestuous wind. The next instant, the stablemaster had been up to his ankles in quicksand, pleading for his life.

"How dare you treat an animal like that? You should be flogged within an inch of your life! Now *I* will dictate the conditions of the sale."

The stablemaster had been in no position to quibble, yielding to her every demand. Her horse was to be sold in the next two days, and if she came back and found it had been mistreated she would personally turn him into a fencepost.

As the adventurer watched the man babble, up to his knees in muck, Ares had marvelled at her skill. It would indeed be better to have this woman as a friend than an enemy! She was a good horse-trader, for not only did she get the horse, but enough feed to keep it for a tenday, along with the wagon and tack, both of which she wanted altered to her exact specifications.

The stablemaster had stammered his agreement as the mud crept over his knees, working its way towards his waist.

With a snap of her fingers the floor solidified, closing around the man's meaty thighs. It had taken the better part of the day to cut him out from his own floor, and most of the night to complete the work on the wagon.

The maid was here now to see its delivery, and the stablemaster had learned his lesson well.

The mare was brought out promptly, looking content and well-fed, and she stomped past him through the stall searching for her stallion. Once assured that he was gone as was the bargain, the maid returned to inspect the wagon. The sides were bright yellow, the struts and trim red and the roof a deep green. If the woman wanted to skip unnoticed out of town, she wouldn't do it in that conveyance.

The healer tested the hinged side that flattened to a shelf and, satisfied, dismissed the stablemaster with a terse nod. The adventurer retreated into a dark shed as the wagon passed, contemplating all he'd seen and heard. When it had rattled around the corner he emerged and, thinking that he'd seen and heard enough, decided to repair to the mainland and wait.

Zelia patted the mare's side. It turned to stare at her placidly, its expression bovine as it chewed away happily on its feed.

"Let's get out of here."

The horse broke wind.

"Just like a cow." She clicked her tongue, trying to get it to move, but it seemed reluctant to leave the shed. She gazed at it for a moment, puzzled, then with a sudden spark of inspiration she visualized a pasture of tall grass interspersed with shady trees. The animal made a sound somewhere between a whinny and a grunt and shuffled apathetically out of the stable.

"Don't you worry, you poor, dumb heifer! I'll have you feeling fit soon enough," she said, and so the horse was dubbed after the beast it most resembled.

By the greasy light of torches and the illumination of four moons, Zelia completed her preparations, rifling through bundles in the old shed behind the boarding house where she lived. After she had stowed everything, she stepped back to survey her work. Her most important possessions – the talismans, amulets and scrolls – fitted easily within the confines of the wagon with room to spare for her pallet.

Then the maid sat, her tongue tucked in the corner of her mouth, as she painted the signs for each of the five moons, the symbols of the seven planets and the gods. She whisked the hair from her face, leaving a long trail of purple on her cheek, dipped the brush into the paint and started on the runes of good fortune. She knew she needed all the protection she could get.

"Well, you're not so high and mighty now, are you, Missus?" said an oily voice from behind her shoulder. Zelia jumped and nearly crossed out the signs for the Bear God Urrl and the Iron God Og.

"Ciril, you old goat! What do you want?"

"Old goat? You ain't going to be so proud when they've stretched your pretty neck for you," the landlord said. He let his head roll to one side and his tongue loll out of his mouth, as he mimed someone holding a rope taut above his head. The whole charade managed to make him look even uglier than usual. He made a gagging noise. "You, with your airs, are too important to pay attention to healers, always off consorting with wizards. Too special to give a bloke the time of day."

"I still won't give you the time of day, old man. Be off with you!"

"You think you're so smart 'cause you gutted a slaver. Maybe you'll be lucky and they won't hang you." The pimply-faced landlord leered at her where she stood amongst the piles of junk, an accumulation of years. "Maybe they'll haul you away and lop off that lovely head of yours."

Zelia shrugged as Ciril eyed the wagon. "And what are you up to? You're not planning to leave us, are you?"

"What's it to you?"

The hunchback drew himself up to his full height, which was still a full head shorter than Zelia. "Why, I'm a law-abiding citizen and it wouldn't do to have a felon evading justice."

"The only thing upstanding about you is . . ."

Somewhere a student shouted and the comment was lost in a boom as an experiment went hopelessly awry. The street behind them disappeared for a moment and then re-materialized, the building fronts painted a garish chequered pattern.

The landlord shied away from her. "No call to get angry at me! I won't give you no trouble, and if you were a bit nicer to me, maybe I could even help you," he whinged.

Zelia stared at him, perplexed, until it dawned on her that he thought she had caused the explosion. "If you don't leave me alone, I'll turn you into a big, fat, pimply toad. Now get out of here!"

He scarpered off, glancing anxiously back at her and then at the weird chequerboard design that was only now starting to fade. When he thought he was far enough away, he spun and shouted, "You can't scare me, you witch! Wait till the hearing, then I'll say my piece. I don't care that they say you can raise the demons of Hades itself. I'll get you!"

As flattering as it was, Zelia could not have raised the denizens from the other planes. Only the fabled Queb could have done that. Besides, who was she to prise them from their business? She returned to her painting. On the morrow she'd be gone, but it really was too bad that she couldn't turn that slimy landlord into a pimply toad before she left.

The blue maid slept little, getting up to prowl the streets uneasily. She played cat and mouse with the fog and the city watch, for this late in the game, it would do no good to call attention to her presence. Dressed in nondescript dun-coloured leather, the maid blended into the background, her bells tucked in a pouch so that their chatter wouldn't betray her.

Without entering them, she stopped at all her old haunts: the Lazy Maiden, the Fat Cleric, the Bitch in the Ditch, and even the bony carcass of the Cock and Boar. As the last moon set, she went back to the shed. After muffling Heifer's hooves, the tack and the wagon's wheels, they set off. Stray wisps of mist eddied around them as Zelia urged the horse silently towards the docks. Here and there, a tallow's flame flared in the window as the butcher and baker prepared to greet the new day. She hoped that no one noticed her passing, but as the wagon rattled away, the landlord stepped from his hiding place and rushed off to get the Special Police.

A golden Pentacle to the ferry captain would ensure that he would suffer from a convenient memory loss should anyone question him. Zelia had considered placing a spell of forgetfulness on him, but magic left its traces. Instead she opted for the universal language of persuasion: money.

Vermilion and gold streaked the sky, and the mist retreated from the wharf as they set sail for the mainland. Zelia leaned on the gaudily painted wagon, using it as a shield against the brisk sea breeze. Lulled by the gentle rocking of the craft, the renegade healer regarded the island's receding shoreline and the life she left behind with dry eyes.

On the pier, the twisted form of Ciril appeared, leaping and gesticulating across the water. Zelia squinted, seeing the fleeing flash of early morning sun off steel, before a merchant moved between her and the ferry's rails and blocked her view.

* * *

Ares had quit the island the previous day. Retreating to the Ticino hills outside the port city, he stationed himself on the highest tor in the city-state of Abruzzi. He stirred the fire as his gaze swept the horizon. In the light of day, Pelopnos could be seen like an emerald embedded in a sea of turquoise, but at this distance, none but the most powerful magic shone even to senses as finely tuned as his. Ares could sense its presence, more as blurring of vision than a light. The area around the island rippled like hot air rising off the deserts of Daklha, and the sky above Thessalia, the city of wizards, pulsed with life. His pupils narrowed to a slit as he stared first at the fuzzy haze that floated over the island of Pelopnos and then at Abruzzi.

No doubt about it, a single strip of flickering magic throbbed over the mainland city.

"Curiouser and curiouser," he said, and his horse stamped and whickered softly in response. The adventurer slipped the bow over his shoulder and slid into the forest to break his fast.

Moving silently as a cat, the warrior pondered the sorcerous trail he had observed. One wizard never radiated that much magic alone, unless he was involved with a great working. Even masters travelling in pairs or in groups did not reveal themselves, unless by visual sighting. Their flamboyant robes gave them away every time.

A hare dashed into the clearing and Ares halted where he stood, arms arrested mid-sweep. The animal hesitated, raised itself on its haunches and sniffed the air, nose twitching furiously while Ares waited, taking this brief pause to reflect on the strange blue maiden. And he wondered idly if the two things were somehow connected.

Seeing nothing, the creature relaxed its vigil and began to dig in the hard earth near the base of a tree. Then Ares fixed his notched bow into position and shot the animal right through its tiny heart. It fell over woodenly and kicked a few times. With a grunt of satisfaction, he retrieved his morning's repast. As he considered the glazing eyes, the mercenary decided that later that day he would remove himself to some place closer to the road.

The ferry docked with a heavy thud and Zelia led Heifer from the deck on to the pier. After stabling the horse, she went immediately to a haberdashery to purchase a capuchin under which she could hide her womanly face and indigo hair. The healer was certain that it had been the hard glimmer of chain mail she had seen as the ferry left Pelopnos wharf. She had hoped her departure would go undetected until the day of the hearing. Perhaps she should have been gentler with that old goat Ciril. Still, she should be safe until the next boat tomorrow, but her looks were distinctive and she saw no reason to tempt fate.

A disguise was required, but she soon discovered that with the loose blouse, leather jerkin and breeches and her head cloaked in the knotted capuchin, few could guess her gender until she spoke. Then brows rose or mouths drooped, but the mere flash of a gold coin usually arrested any further inquiries about her odd appearance and even odder attire.

Markers were no problem. Her father provided a generous allowance, paid in silver and brass, even gold, that befitted her station as the daughter of an immortal and a sheik, and her stepmother the Lady Hadidge added a princely sum to his bequest in return for Zelia's continued absence from her father's tents. But the maid clung fiercely to each coin, knowing it to be the last stipend she would see for quite some time. Once in the city centre, she needed to pick up those provisions she hadn't been able to purchase in Thessalia. At each shop, Zelia would wave a golden Pentacle under the shopkeeper's nose before pocketing it quickly. Then the owner would follow her around the store, encouraging her to buy this or that and hoping to get his hands on the Pentacle and, if not that, at least as many markers as she was willing to part with.

First, there was food: the thick black stimulant drink, *cha*; dragonpears, a tangy fruit so named because they tended to bite back; apples; dried fruit; hard cheeses and rugged travellers' cake. Then she purchased pots and utensils for the making of meals and brews.

In Alchemist's Lane, she bought those herbs she would be unlikely to find along the road and stocked up on essential oils and valuable spices. Browsing through the shops in Wizard's Row, Zelia discovered, to her delight, a firemaker's wand. As she stared longingly at it through the window she could have sworn it smiled at her and the sale was made on the spot.

At Liar's Square, she bought trinkets and baubles which she could sell to the uninitiated as talismans and amulets. From the ragman, she got cloth to be used for bandages and pouches. At an inn, she purchased a barrel of *kumys*, a fermentation of mares' milk, and *kvass*, along with empty bottles and a battered old funnel.

Pausing long enough to feed Heifer, Zelia

noticed the stablemaster talking to a member of the local watch and heard mention of the fire at the old Cock and Boar. She sidled closer to listen, but the conversation soon passed to other things and she breathed a sigh of relief.

Absentmindedly, the maid held on to an apple for Heifer. The horse nibbled it, her breath moist on Zelia's palm, and the healer contemplated her next move. Perhaps it was time to put some distance between herself and Abruzzi. As the scarlet moon crested the horizon, they were clattering down the road away from the city.

Queb squinted at the smoke that issued from the Devil's mouth. It was handy to have a demon in your pocket, he thought.

On that foggy canvas, the demon painted a picture of the outside world. When the wizard focused, the image would change and Queb could then observe selected visions. But a demon is an untrustworthy ally, and today it wouldn't summon the one face he most desired. His gazed shifted from the foul vapour to the creature's writhing features.

This particular demon had come uninvited to the wizard's aid, and it demanded a rich harvest of human souls for its services. But what did Queb care that it would release a plague upon the land? What was it to him, a few meagre mortal souls for the satan to toy with? Nothing mattered to Queb except the grand design. He could spare a few human lives. When he ruled, he wouldn't miss them much. Even the maid was only a stepping stone in his plan, but the revenge that would be inflicted on the mother with the woman's final demise made this task twice as sweet.

Queb cackled, coughed, and motioned for the demon to scan forward through the planes. Mortal land turned to snow and then settled on the flickering fairy as she flapped frantically around the chuckling fountain.

"Lost," she moaned and her despair echoed endlessly about the stone circle. A look of bewilderment crossed her almost transparent features, and the necromancer realized that she probably couldn't remember what she was seeking.

The twitter deepened to a guffaw, and Queb found breath enough in his hollow shell to bellow his mirth. Soon his time would come and he would be avenged. Then he would be released from his self-imposed prison, but for now he could watch and wait. He had an entire mountain empire and his creations to do his bidding. His powers grew stronger daily, even if his body was still weak.

With a crackle, the picture changed and Queb was staring into the bone-thin face of the Matriarch. With her hawk nose, sunken features and elaborate crown, she looked like a crude scarecrow with an inflated sense of self-worth. He concentrated on the fiend's spectral cloud, stooping closer to the image and scowling.

He remembered her vaguely. Surely the Devil's imp had a reason for showing him this? Inspiration struck. Every adversary had its weak link, and perhaps the wizard had found the girl's. Queb couldn't get at the mother, but maybe the father . . .

The wizard pointed at the Matriarch and she glanced up from her work in the herbarium, scratched her head, knocking the headdress askew, and hurried off unwittingly to do his bidding.

The Matriarch wrote furiously, the quill pen scratching along the parchment. When the message was complete, she leaned back to survey her work. The letter to the sheik was terse, and she wondered now if it was a very good idea to tell him of Zelia's change in status and her subsequent disappearance. Then she shrugged with a jingle of bells and the faint tinkling of crystal cloth. The father had a right to know if for no other reason than to stop the subsidy he provided for his daughter's maintenance. And who knew whether or not he had a spy secreted somewhere in her halls? Most nobles did that sort of thing, planting spies in every major court and temple. The lesser the nobility, the more likely they were to have a vast system of spies spreading across the two continents. And a terem eunuch could move easily undetected among the staff. No, it was better that the sheik should hear it from her.

The Matriarch secured the missive with her seal and summoned a messenger, eyeing the tall eunuch, whose name she could not recall. She gave him the parchment along with instructions that it be taken to the tent of Sheik Al Y Kazzam, wherever it might be found deep in the Shamirian desert.

"The witch has been excommunicated, Lord," said the Inquisitor. "Should we pursue her?"

"An excommunicated healer? Ha! What harm can she do?" The Archmage coughed and waved at the cloud of torch smoke that surrounded him.

" 'Tis said she exhibited powers that were truly awesome that night."

"Bah! With so many spells flying, who can tell who did what to whom?" the Archmage said. "We still haven't found the proper ingredients to turn Simon from a pig. That cock-up took the mangling of more than one spell. Who's to say that the enchantments attributed to the girl did not come from some ardent admirer? I hear she was a pretty young thing despite her ancestry," the mage added, circumspectly. "No, let the civil authorities take care of her. We shouldn't sully our hands with some miscreant halfling."

The yellow and red wagon bounced down the rutted road away from Abruzzi. The area was populous and the land much cultivated, with few places to hide. Zelia risked a hurried peep over her shoulder and winced when she recognized the bright livery of the Pelopnos Special Police.

Already the law was on her tail, and she was barely one step ahead of them. She urged Heifer to a trot. The mare pranced like a pony, and Zelia noted with satisfaction that the animal was starting to fill out and her coat had grown glossy and sleek. Still, the pace was too much for the poor creature. The horse chuffed, its sides heaving with the effort. They would have to stop soon.

"I'm sorry, Heifer. Just make it around the next bend and we'll hide," she murmured to the straining beast. She had expected more time to make good her escape.

They rounded the curve and the uniformed officers disappeared from view. She drove the wagon into the brush and jumped out of her seat to scatter dry leaves over the wheelmarks.

As she heard the jingle of bridles and the clang of arms, Zelia called upon reserves of power she did not know she had and whispered a fade spell. The outline of both wagon and horse softened and faded and the next thing she knew she could see the gaunt shadows of trees through Heifer's heaving sides. In a second both wagon and beast were gone, and Zelia looked about her frantically. The glen was sparsely wooded, and no power on earth could magic her away.

The guard argued loudly. "I told you she bought the wagon. My cousin's the stable-master, you see. She threatened his life. What could he do? She had him paint it special, and *that*," he paused for emphasis, "was the wagon. Who but a sorceress would have the bad taste to paint it yellow, red and green? You saw it. We'll have her in our hands before teatime."

"I saw it, but I don't believe it. No fugitive in his right mind would paint a wagon red, yellow and green."

"She's half elemental." The other guard spoke as if that explained such vulgarity.

All was lost. She hadn't expected them to follow so soon. Silver spear tips gleamed as they started around the bend.

"Pssst," a voice hissed from somewhere above her head. She glanced up at the pale face of a little boy.

"Up here!" he said.

She climbed into the tree.

"Inside," the boy said, indicating something that looked like a squirrel's nest. "It's bigger than it looks."

Zelia climbed across the limb and dived into the leafy door. She was brought up short by three eager faces that regarded her. Pressing herself against the woven wall, she pulled her knees up to her chest to make room for her rescuer.

He squirmed into the entrance. There was barely enough room for all of them. The boy signalled the group to silence, and Zelia examined the children before her. Two girls, with hair the colour of summer corn and two boys, dark-haired and slender. Beneath them, unseen guards continued to quarrel.

"Well, where is she?"

"I don't know. She must be up ahead."

"Maybe she magicked herself away."

"No wizard can do that!"

"What makes you think you know what

wizards can do? Don't tell me you've got a cousin who's a wizard too."

The armour and tack clattered loudly and the quibbling continued. The voices retreated into the distance, and Zelia let out a long, low exhalation.

The second boy shook his head and she nodded in agreement. If they could still hear the soldiers, then the soldiers could probably hear them. A hush descended on the group, until the clop of metal-shod feet was just a jangling memory, and the smallest girl spoke. "Can we talk now?"

"They're gone," the second girl added.

"Of course," said the eldest boy with an air of command, as he wriggled towards the leafy exit. Zelia followed and, one by one, they dropped to the ground.

"And who might my rescuers be?"

"I'm Brendan," said the first boy.

"I'm Michael," said the second, "and that's Lisa and Emily."

A whinny interrupted the introductions. Zelia peered at Heifer, who stood like a ghostly image against the harsh outline of trees. Already the wagon was growing more solid. The spell hadn't held for long.

"Come with us. You can hide at our house for the night," said Lisa.

"And there's room in the barn for the wagon," said Brendan. Zelia stared down the road in the direction of the unseen Pelopnos Special Police and nodded.

Let them search ahead. Once the area had been investigated it was unlikely that they would check it again, and then she would be safe to travel on. That night the young girls smuggled food to their strange guest, and she told them stories to keep them entertained. She and Heifer slept surrounded by the sweet smell of warm hay. The next day Zelia took her leave of her small saviours, but she remembered their names each night in her prayers.

The country became more rugged as they neared the border. All five moons bloomed fat and swollen in the heavens – a rare occurrence – each tinted with the five hues of healing: purple, yellow, red, blue and green. Zelia examined the night sky. They had almost joined in a most fortuitous conjunction. She studied them more closely. It would be exact in the next two rotations.

With that thought, she reined in the plodding Heifer. This was as good a place to settle as any. To her left was a copse which would provide ample cover. With a groan, Zelia massaged her aching rear and climbed down from her seat, guiding Heifer towards the trees. They pushed into the woods, going deeper and deeper, until she found a single standing stone that pointed a jagged finger at the interlaced branches above her head.

This would do nicely.

She ducked into the wagon and fished through the many scrolls until she found the one marked with a half-crescent and another that appeared to be slashed with a series of random lines. She unrolled the latter and revealed a map of the ley-line grid. As she flattened it out, the fire wand tumbled next to her feet. She had quite forgotten about it.

Ah, yes, a fire to see by, she thought.

Zelia scooped the wand from the ground and went to gather wood and twigs, then she sat on a stone and studied the wand. She could have sworn it was grinning at her.

"So, how do you work?"

The wand stared back at her, silent and intractable.

She gestured towards the tinder and said simply, "Fire!" The wand flared for a minute and then dimmed, becoming darker than the surrounding forest.

"Look you," she shook it, "I'm tired, I'm irritable, and I've been on the run for days. You'll give me fire without further ado or you'll be nothing more than so much glittering dust."

The glass wand seemed to – if such a thing were possible – scrunch down on itself stubbornly. She could almost imagine it crossing tiny arms and tapping an invisible toe at her. She shook it again.

"Don't think I wouldn't," she said. "I've got a hammer in there," she inclined her head towards the wagon, "and the temper to do it!"

The firemaker's wand blazed. With a sharp cry, she dropped it and it bounced off the ground. Lightning flashed around the grove, lighting limb and dry leaves, and the wand was gone in a puff of smoke.

Around her, light shone blindingly off the wagon's bright yellow sides, green roof and flaming scarlet trim. Zelia whispered a quick cool spell she often used to heal a patient of burns, and ice crystals formed in the air around the grove. They melted rapidly and rain began to fall with a sizzling hiss on the trees above her head. A fire leapt cheerily in her makeshift grate.

Zelia grimaced. It would be several days before she found the wand sulking inside a scroll of firemakers' spells. "Perhaps I should have spoken to it more politely," she muttered quietly to herself.

Then the maid bent to study the maps before

her, her finger tracing a ley line from Thessalia to her current position next to the solitary standing stone where several lines merged. She smiled; this place was perfect.

Even after several days' travel, Greybeard Tor was still visible. The grizzled granite head canted towards a curious pillar of stone that stretched straight up to the heavens. A bridge spanned the gap between tilting tor and column, giving the appearance of some doddering old man leaning against his stick.

A skinned hoary marmoset bubbled and spat gaily on Ares' spit while its purple skin hung to dry from a limb. He could get a few clay markers for it at the next village.

Ares lifted his head and peered into the distance. Orange-red light bounced crazily somewhere to the west. His warhorse shifted nervously and he turned to look at it.

So this radiance was visible to all, even a poor, dumb beast.

When the young man's gaze returned to survey the silver road that twisted languidly from the Tor through the hills, like a white cat wrapping itself round the old man's ankles, the sky above him was again illuminated only by the five moons.

The next day, Zelia positioned wards around the small clearing, etching runes in the hard soil. According to her map, the standing stone marked a place of special magic, a minor joining of the lines along the grid. Its proximity would strengthen the potency of her brews. She set her pots to boiling and went to gather the additional herbs she needed. The sweet fragrance of starfire leaf and velvet flower mingled with acrid aroma of grandfather's foot, a root so named because it smelled a lot like the inside of an old man's boots.

The glen grew misty and hot, the steam held in by the wards. Zelia mixed the ingredients to create come-hither oils, anointing oils, wealth and prosperity oils, oils for the many gods, and oils to ward off evil spirits and ill-will. As the pots bubbled, she made sachets and simples: for love, for health and happiness, and for protection from real and imagined foes.

Until she finished her quest, the healer would have to support herself in some way, and she fully intended to ply her trade, studiously avoiding the cities and keeping to the countryside. She'd work as a travelling mountebank, peddling her wares and curing what ills she could.

Zelia stirred the brews, pouring them into the bottles she had purchased, and then chose names for them. Universal Specific, Og's Rejuvenator and Ullr's Tonic. The first was a sedative, the second a stimulant, and the last had an analgesic effect. Made of soothing herbs and liberally spiked with *kumys* and *kvass*, they did no harm. In fact, they had a certain nutritive value and made the recipient feel a little bit better, no matter what ailed him.

The rota of the moons' conjunction was nigh. Rarely did all the moons appear at one time, much less abide next to each other in their celestial home. Usually, they would travel along pre-set paths low across the heavens and far from their sisters, no more than three moons at a time. For the five sisters and daughters of Brigitta were a quarrelsome lot. When they did journey close to each other, they didn't so much rest as collide. It was a day of great magic.

Zelia chose that day to place small magicks on the glittering trinkets, baubles, and beads to create amulets. Nothing stupendous – only trifling enchantments. On one old silver spoon, she cast a fruitfulness spell so that it would provide its bearer with one kingly meal. The owner's faith would do the rest, for Zelia knew that small magicks were largely sustained by belief. Put simply, if one believed, the object worked. The matrix itself would work only once, but by then the seed would be planted, and if the bearer had any magic of his own, it would continue to function as intended.

The maid laboured feverishly. Time was short, and she felt the need to get away, to flee this place so close to the Isle of Learning. Although the search had passed her by, she knew herself to be in danger still. She sensed that she was being followed, but could find no proof to credit such a conviction – a fluttering branch, a waving twig, no more. Zelia shivered despite the sun which dappled the scorched boughs above her head.

Besides, this close to the college, the wizards' magic could still be felt. As long as they and their workings remained nearby, she could not possibly sense another magician's hand. She did not know where Queb was hiding, but she was reasonably sure that it wouldn't be anywhere near Ticino, a place which he too would wish to avoid.

When the last glittering rock or broken bit of jewellery had been bewitched Zelia broke camp, eager to be away from the place. As soon as she released the wards, a shadowy figure appeared – a guard of the Pelopnos Special Police, his throat cut in a second smile. Zelia could see the stone through his gauzy form.

A ghost. His soul so newly released from the flesh that he had yet to make his way to the immortal planes.

He stared at her with empty eyes and wailed. "Beware," he said, "of the one with snow-white hair. Oh, treachery! Ware! Ware the one with a heart of ice!"

Heifer reared, and Zelia had to cover the mare's eyes and lead her away from the guard as he continued to wail his warning into empty space.

The adventurer writhed in his sleep. He walked the Dream Fields, a place of snow and ice. The scene throbbed in unblemished white, and he was temporarily blinded. Then his vision was filled with the face of the most beautiful woman he had ever seen. Her hair was the colour of moonbeams. She clasped him in her arms and he squirmed like a child impatient to be free. She took a single step, and the world turned to brown. Stones – their flanks covered with hairy lichen, their tops broken like jagged teeth – surrounded them on all four sides. Unimpressed, he played with the snowy strands of the woman's hair. She moved swiftly through the circle and bent to place her now silent youngster on his feet.

"Your place, my child, is here for now, but I will be waiting for you. When you can find your way safely through the mists, you can return."

Ares trembled.

"Don't worry, child – already your mentor comes. He will help you. He will give you all that he has and more."

Bang, bang, bang, bang!

The woman vanished, and Ares was roused from his light doze. He scanned the small camp, wondering fuzzily what had awakened him. The road was to his right. He had stopped within sight of the spot where he had seen light glittering among the trees two nights ago. The magical strand which had seemed so clear during the previous three rotations had disappeared, and he felt like one blind.

There was a muffled thump, a yelp, and someone swore beyond by the grove. Ares got up and made a wide circle around the sound. Through a break in the trees he could see two officers of the Special Police, one trying clumsily to tack a poster on to the spiny surface of a fire oak with the help of a rock.

"Hurry up, will ya?" the other grumbled.

"Don't rush me. We're almost through. I've only got a couple more, and I'd like to keep as many fingers as I can. I've already smashed three," the first said. "What's the hurry anyway?"

"There's a good public house up the road and I'd like to be there when it opens. It's a fool's errand; the wench is long gone by now."

"You're right and this is thirsty work. I'll be ready in the twinkling of a gnat's eye."

Ares retired further into dense brush. The guard gave the poster a gentle tug to see if it was secure and picked up the remaining two posters. They left, and the adventurer crept from his hiding place to examine the picture. Occasionally he earned a few markers as a bounty hunter, and he had to admit his purse was getting a bit thin.

Ares beheld the familiar face.

He read it: "Wanted for murder and illicit witchery. Considered armed and dangerous."

"Surprise, surprise!" he sniggered.

Chewing on his lip, Ares gazed on the fragile features and turned away. Then he hesitated and swung back to tear the poster from its perch. Folding it neatly, the mercenary placed it in his pocket, patted it and smiled. Checking to see if his mount was secured, he slithered through the trees. Moving parallel to the road, he halted only long enough to tear the rest of the posters down. Otherwise, his pace did not falter until he was back within range of the guards' voices. He trailed like a wraith behind them as one man boasted his prowess with a local dairy maid. Listening to his tale, the adventurer snorted. He doubted if the man spoke true. Ares had learned from his mentor that those who swaggered most usually had the least to brag about.

Ares tracked them to the public house and followed them inside. He hung back to watch them as they ordered and settled at a table. Investing the last of his funds, he bought three drinks – two more of the same and one for himself – and went to join them.

Their eyes flicked from the belt to the weapons to his face, and they blenched. Their manner was cold, but they warmed as soon as they saw the drinks. The mercenary extracted the poster from his pocket and passed it to them.

"Tell me about the girl," he said, and they hunched over their mugs happy to oblige.

Several hours later, they stumbled from the tavern dead-drunk. Their arms linked in friendly camaraderie, they followed a reeling course back towards Abruzzi. Suddenly the guard called Hector stopped, weaving where he stood. He belched, groaned, put his hand over his mouth and ran for the side of the road.

His mate Giovi chortled. "Can't hold your drink, hey, mate?" He swayed a bit, a look of concentration on his face. "Come to think of it," he said, "I need to get rid of a little liquid myself. I'll be back in a bit."

As he disappeared through the trees, Ares abandoned the soft, unfocused expression of the inebriate, and his face hardened as he considered Hector, who was retching into the bushes with loud whooping noises. The man would be busy for a while yet, and so Ares went loping after Giovi, who was tottering noisily through the woods.

His step was arrested by the soft patter of water on the ground. The mercenary's eyes were drawn to a pale flame that flickered in the distance somewhere beyond the guard. The man grunted and began to rearrange jerkin, mail and cloak. Ares glided around him, unheard and unseen, and headed for the flickering light.

At that moment the guard also noticed the capering campfire and began blundering through the underbrush, sounding like a whole herd of furry mammoths. Ares was just about to hiss him to silence when a figure unfolded into view, and the adventurer couldn't believe his luck.

Or his misfortune. Somewhere behind him, Ares heard a gasp as Giovi recognized their quarry. Any second now, the fool would raise the alarm. Then Ares realized that the guard had not yet noticed his presence. The mercenary bolted, melting swift and silent as a shade into the trees.

Giovi pulled his shield from his back and started to draw his blade. The sword had not completely cleared the scabbard when Ares sprung forward and slit the man's throat, catching his body as it deflated with a bubbling gurgle into his arms. He lowered the corpse gently to the ground, his eyes fixed on the maiden as she stirred the bubbling cauldron, stretched luxuriously and then lay down. Before he had loosed his grip from Giovi, her body went limp and slack. The next thing Ares knew, he felt a small probing on his forehead, between his eyes. He clamped down hard, silencing his thoughts, and the fleeting touch was gone.

Leaving the guard where he lay, Ares hurried back to the road to take care of his partner.

Sheik Al Y Kazzam lolled lazily on the soft cushions of satin and silk embroidered with gold. He liked life among his many wives. This one gentled him and that one coddled him. He would have laughed if he had heard the Matriarch's assessment of nobility and spies, for nothing could be further from his mind. Ever since the sheik had stumbled into the stone circle and got lost between the planes, the tall handsome nobleman preferred the silken tents of the sprawling terem to his male court. His trip to fabled lands had changed him irrevocably, and although he was still a skilled swordsman, he shunned his warriors. Some said he was losing his grip on reality, for he showed a maiden's mercy, dismissing an adversary rather than fighting him. Proof of his insanity came with his acceptance of the half-breed daughter and his permissiveness with her.

Of all his children, the sheik loved Zelia best. He couldn't even remember the names of all the others, except a favoured son or two. But Zelia had defied tradition and graced his tents with her dazzling smile and musical laugh. And she was so like her mother. He loved the child more because of her fay mother's illusiveness, for of all the women the sheik had desired, only Zelia's mother had eluded him.

The sheik's face clouded for a moment as he tried to recollect the Lady Astra's image. Whenever he thought of her, she would spring spritely to mind, a vision that would swiftly pale and shred, floating like tattered dust motes in the sun, until he could not have described a single feature to anyone.

His daughter too was lost to him, banished to a far land, and he missed her dearly. He could not blame her if she did not want to marry the fat Emir. She was right; he *did* look like a ton of quivering lard. With her ability for mischief, he doubted that she would have survived her wedding night. She would have done something wrong, said something wrong, and her head would have been forfeit.

The sheik sighed and the Lady Hadidge clapped her hands, waving the dancing girl away.

"That one does not please you, my lord? Perhaps . . ." And she gestured at another just as a guard appeared, his head stuck inside the tent flap, his eyes carefully averted. The sheik thought he recognized him – some cousin or other – but then in the Kazzam clan they were all cousins. The ladies scattered with genteel shrieks. Others cringed, lifting shimmering veils to cover their exposed faces.

The sheik rolled his eyes at the ceiling of the large tent. "Come in. Come in."

Staring at his feet, the warrior shuffled forward. "A message for you from the Healers' College." He held the sealed scroll tightly clenched in his fist and offered it to the sheik as though it were a magical charm.

"Ah, a letter from Zelia. Bring it here," the sheik beckoned to the guard. "And don't trip over your own feet. By the gods, man, watch what you are doing! You've seen a woman before."

All this hoopla was so silly. If only Zelia were here now, she'd get the best of him. She'd thrust her face into his and tweak his beard until he looked at her.

The sheik took the scroll from the man's trembling fingers and, relieved, the guard scurried from the curtained terem chamber.

"Fool!" Kazzam muttered as he broke the seal and flattened the parchment, peering at it owlishly for a moment before jumping to his feet.

"This is an outrage!" he bellowed.

The Lady Hadidge flinched and sighed. *What had the child done now?*

"Summon my steed! Send for my steward and tell him to gather my things, and have the vizier notify the captain of my fastest sea-going vessel to prepare for voyage. I set off today for Pelopnos," he shouted as he stormed towards the open flap.

The Lady Hadidge touched his hand. "My lord, what has happened?"

"The insult!" he fumed. "Zelia has been expelled! I must go and fetch her home. She will become court healer, damn them! She has more power in her little finger than they have in the whole enclave."

He tore through the door and the flap – window to the women's world – closed behind him.

The Lady Hadidge settled in a flurry of chaste black cloth – suitable for a chief wife and concubine – a look of dread on her face. She was not surprised that the girl had been expelled – only that it had taken so long. She wondered if she could have prevented it. *Perhaps if she had sent them a few more bangles, some more tempting beads . . .*

Zelia hastened north, ever northward. Each night she'd cast about her, seeking the dread presence and following the sour reek of evil. Each day she became more and more convinced that someone pursued her still. She sensed the presence as one of shimmering white, and cold! So very cold. Sometimes she wanted to run, but she did not, unsure if the one she sought to shun was the one she should in fact be seeking.

Her stalker's spirit hovered around the edge of the Dream Fields, but he kept it shrouded so that she could not read him to tell whether he was friend or foe. During the day he followed her, and Zelia would note his passing in the bending of a branch and the slight rustling of dead leaves.

The small caravan moved in fits and starts along the eastern side of the mountain range. As the days lengthened into early spring, Zelia didn't stray too far from her camp, and always settled close to some dwelling. She did not want to be alone.

Already her nightly search had yielded another member of the Special Police who was pursuing her. Zelia had almost tripped over the blurred thoughts of a blundering guard as he dragged his weary body home from the fruitless hunt. In his jumbled mind, she sensed fatigue and anger at this quest to bring a healer to the rack. All it took then was a little mental nudge to persuade him to hurry and tarry no longer so far from his hearth. A forgetfulness spell the following morning, and the object of his quest conveniently slipped his mind. That had been easy, but the healer shuddered to think what would happen to her if she ran into someone more determined – someone without a new wife and an even newer babe awaiting his return.

Everywhere Zelia went she found ills, big and small – sniffles, sneezes, a racking cough, festering wounds, boils and abscesses. Each cottage, it seemed, had its aches and its hurts. In one village, Zelia brought a young man out of an enchanted slumber, and it was rumoured she could raise the dead. For the first time the young woman understood some of the Matriarch's rage at being separated from the people who needed the healers most. Cloistered at the temple and before that in the terem, she'd never seen such suffering, and Zelia swore that when she took over the Crown of Brigitta the system would change.

As temple messenger, Zelia had travelled far, from garrisoned castle to foppish palace. She had met the Potentate of Uri, the Queen of Shalop, the King of the Norvons and the Tzar of Szatmar. She'd discussed the controversies of the day with the nobility of every country where the order had stationed a healer. Under the Matriarch's tutelage, Zelia had learned politics and guile. But even then she had been cloistered in some stuffy old court with its rigid disciplines and stifling protocol. And she decided she preferred this simpler life, where she was unfettered and free.

The maid accepted nothing for her treatment. She made enough on her sales, so she kept her vows as best she could. Often, though, the patient would press payment on her, and she took no more than she thought the person could afford – a bunch of onions, some fresh herbs or grain for Heifer. A tinker, whose arm she had set, made her a large bell which she tolled when she arrived at each new village. One farmer, whose son's life she had saved, tried to give her a pig but Zelia refused, settling instead for a chicken, and the bird became her travelling companion.

The hen she called Flighty, and Zelia decided that as friends go Heifer and Flighty were all she needed. They didn't complain when she returned to the camp late, or stumbled home weaving and legless. She wore her bells openly, advertising her vocation, and was welcomed, fed and applauded – with plenty of liquid spirits for the asking and lusty youths to keep her company. So Zelia was content, or as content as she could be with evil luring her forward and a mysterious presence hanging behind.

The delicate braceleted hand shredded the white lichen that grew in such abundance here near the Uri–Norvon border. Zelia sprinkled the slow-burning fungus over the campfire. It would dampen the fire without completely suffocating the flames. A few glowing embers would remain in the morning, and she could revive these with a handful of dry tinder, a stir of a stick, or a rudimentary spell.

The spacious cart could no longer house her so Zelia made her bed outside under the silvery light of the stars. A gentle wind filtered through the trees. Heifer, nose stuffed in a bag, munched contentedly, and Flighty sat staring broodily at her mistress, red-eyed in the reflected light of the fire.

The young woman scanned the thin shrubs, alert for signs of danger. A large oak provided a little cover and a boulder sheltered her back. She settled back and felt the reassuring weight of the large brass bell of office nestled between her breasts. Normally it sounded with the clear treble of middle C, but it had been silenced until she could take her place at the Matriarch's side. She missed its sweet tone. The chirp of F sharp rose from her ankle. She savoured the note, reciting its attributes out loud and recalling what part of man's body it penetrated and what ailments it cured, using rote memorization to lull her.

Then Zelia slumped and sent forth her spirit. She grasped the rays of stars and moons, riding the breeze, until ephemeral feet rested on the shadowy path of the grid. Thunder and lightning battled far away in the southeast, but the maid turned from it, knowing it to be no threat to her. Her mind's eye swung to the north, towards the frozen wastes, where it appeared that the ley wavered, its lines wiggling drunkenly. When Zelia tried to tread these reeling strands, she was wrapped in the sticky cords of pure sorcery. Frightened, she struggled like a fly trapped in a spider's web.

Suddenly, she was enveloped in a blaze of white light. The snarling web froze and splintered, falling to earth with a sound like the pattering tinkle of ice shards, and Zelia was left alone, floating in the heavens above her camp. From her position among the clouds, she saw nothing save a few scattered fires where others had rested from their day's travels. She sensed only weariness – no peril, either natural or supernatural, nor even the residual aura of ill-intent. She descended back into her body.

Her eyes opened and she stretched, knowing now that her path was north still, and took the time to delight in the silvery comfort of the stars and moons before she slipped into the sweet slumber of oblivion.

Queb roared with rage as the white light seared across the dark strand of his enchantment and severed his contact with the maid. For weeks he had urged her on, drawing her tighter into the web. Her powers were untrained and undeveloped. She couldn't even sense his hovering spirit, unless he wanted her to, and tonight he almost had her. He had lured her to his treacherous trap. One more minute and he could have crushed her like a bug.

Foiled!

The wizard raised a withered fist at the heavens. He would deal with the fairy whelp some other way, for without doubt she knew where he was now, and she would come hurrying in this direction.

Again the warrior hunted his prey through the Dream Fields. Below him, the ley-line grid radiated dully. Ares sensed movement and followed. The next thing he knew, he was caught between two wills, immobilized in the sticky bonds of enchantment. They battled on around him, unaware of his presence.

Anger flared, and he was a child again, helpless as others decided his future for him.

He jerked awake next to a dying fire sitting upright. He lowered himself again into the soft bracken that made his bed. His body still tingled. He tossed and turned on the hard ground and waited for sleep to find him, but it did not find him.

With a grunt of disgust, he stood and prepared to break camp. Slumber would not visit him again this night. It was time to move on and, he was thinking, about time he got answers to a few of his questions.

The rustle of cloth and a soft footfall woke Zelia two hours later. Instantly vigilant, she surveyed the scene before her with half-closed eyes. Two stockinged legs were silhouetted by the glowing embers. Beyond those, another pair straddled her pack. Hovering somewhere above her head and barely within her line of vision, she saw the hem of a rich brocade riding-coat. Without moving, she mentally gauged the distance to her sword. One leg of the closer pair lifted and took a stealthy step forward, and Zelia lunged.

Many things happened simultaneously as she grasped her blade and rose in a single fluid motion. A hitherto unseen man leapt between herself and the young velvet-clad brigand. Surprised, the thief flinched, his sword half-in and half-out of his scabbard. His brocaded partner, however, was quicker, withdrawing his sword and feinting as the first recovered his wits. With a strident clatter of bells Zelia darted past the unknown third man and spun in a two-handed sweep. She pinked the youth but did not press her advantage, her attention split between her assailant and her would-be rescuer. From the corner of her eye, she watched as he parried easily with the other brigand. She saw him thrust his point home, the tip of his rapier stopping just short of the young man's ribs.

The blackguard dropped his weapon and raised his hands in surrender, and Zelia wondered what her so-called rescuer would do next. The soft whizz of a blade next to her ear caught her attention. With a shout of fury and frustration, the healer whirled, catching the other man's sword with the tip of her own. A deft twist and she wrested the lighter weapon from the brigand's grip, heaving it far into the brush. The youth stood stock still, mouth agape.

Holding her sword to the robber's throat, she wheeled to assess her rescuer and stopped the gasp before it escaped her lips. The man dipped his sword in a show of respect and sheathed it, and Zelia turned to her assailants, whom she judged from their attire to be younger sons of nobility, typically dissolute and cowardly. They stood, chins drooping as though they hoped to catch an early-morning moth, and much bemused by the appearance of a sword-wielding cleric who wore the healer's bells.

"Get out, and leave the sword." She dismissed them with an imperious wave of her hand, and they scarpered off without debate.

Her rescuer leaned against a large tree, arms crossed, his casual stance belied by his wary expression. She returned his scrutiny with a measured examination of her own. Her gaze flicked immediately to his hair, and she took an involuntary step backwards.

Ware, the ghost had said, *the man with snow-white hair.*

The thick silver mane was twined in a single braid which hung down a well-muscled body. He was tall, towering several handspans above her head, and lissom. His jerkin and leggings were of soft Ticino leather, and he was armed to the teeth. Besides the small sword, a sheathed dagger was strapped to his arm, and the battle hammer of Og – as deadly as any mace – hung at his back. Around his waist, he wore a belt of human scalps. An icy hand clutched at Zelia's heart. The slightly slanted, cold blue eyes and narrow face revealed an ancestry as mixed as her own. He was most likely a snow elf, judging from his colouring, and she pondered the white wraith who had chased her through this realm and the next. Zelia suppressed a shiver as she replaced her sword.

"My name is Zelia," she said. "I suppose I should thank you."

"I'm Ares," he bowed formally to her. "No thanks are necessary. I suspect you could have disarmed them yourself. You handle a blade well." With a sharp jut of his chin, he indicated her sword and sheath as she slung it across her back. "An unusual accoutrement for a healer, don't you think?"

Her order eschewed weapons of death. Only the messengers were exempt, since it might be necessary for a cleric to defend herself along the road, and Zelia, as the Matriarch's personal messenger, had often travelled abroad armed.

The Sword of Brigitta was considered sacred. Cooled in the Temple's waters, the messenger's blade could heal an injury as well as inflict one. Long and unwieldy, it was made to protect its messenger owner from horseback. The blade was too clumsy to wear and would easily have tangled in her legs. So the saddle for the messenger of Brigitta was made with a built-in sheath.

The saddle was long gone, but the habit was ingrained. Zelia went armed. As the Matriarch's special apprentice, she had been taught to ignore tradition, and in her current position she knew that rules were made to be broken, or at least bent, especially when it meant girding her person against potential danger.

Zelia kept both her blades – her Shamirian scimitar and Brigitta's sacred sword – within easy reach. From the back of a destrier or standing on the Goddess's good earth, Zelia could wield either the lighter scimitar or the ungainly sword with agility, as well as the most accomplished swordsman. And she had designed a sheath that fastened across her shoulders and back, similar to the leather device from which Ares' hammer hung.

The maiden sniffed her contempt at his

question. "A woman travelling alone must be prepared to defend herself. One cannot play the coy damsel, or call upon the Blessed Brigitta when a man has a knife at one's throat."

Motioning towards the path along which her unwelcome guests had fled, she commented wryly, "Your arrival is timely and unexpected. I didn't hear you come. Do you have a horse?"

He pointed to the brush in the thicket beyond and nodded. "I hope you didn't skewer the poor beast when you tossed the lad's sword."

"Sorry, I didn't know."

"There wasn't much time for chit-chat." Ares stooped to stir the fire.

"What brings you out so late?" Zelia glanced up at the sky. The last moon had set and the first faint promise of dawn gilded the horizon. "Or perhaps I should say so early."

"I felt a stirring on the winds."

Her bells jingled softly, and she gave him a sidelong glance.

"A stirring?" she asked nonchalantly as she watched him play with the fire.

He shrugged. "I feel naught now. It was nothing. Only a dream."

"Or maybe an ill-wind?" Zelia said as she went to the wagon. Returning, she handed him cheese and rough black bread. "So what do you do when you aren't rescuing damsels in distress?"

"A bit of this, a bit of that." He busied himself fanning the flames as she squatted beside him, gnawing on a dragonpear.

As Ares teased the glowing coals into a cheery blaze, she leaned closer, poking at his belt. "That is strange raiment. Why do you adorn yourself with the scalps of others?"

"This? It is the hair of unbelievers. You might say it is part of my quest," he chuckled unpleasantly.

"Quest?" she raised a single brow, adding with a little sarcasm of her own, "How romantic!"

Ares snorted. "Hardly."

She tugged at one of the scalps and turned to him, questioning.

"It belonged to my master. He bequeathed it to me when he died."

"Master? You were a slave?"

"Not really, but I don't know what else to call him. He wasn't my father. He found me abandoned when I was nothing but a sprig and he took me in. A follower of Og, he gave me this," Ares clutched the belt at his waist, "when he died and commanded me to carry on his work of converting non-believers."

Zelia shuddered. "Seems a trifle heavy-handed, don't you think?"

"Yes, even his fellow members thought his method of persuasion extreme. He was excommunicated, or whatever you call it. He wasn't a bad sort, I don't suppose. I think he was lonely, and that's why he kept me around."

Zelia shivered. "And have you been successful with your quest?"

Ares leaned back and guffawed. "Oi, woman, do you think I'm mad? I keep the belt. It was all he left me besides my name." He went on, with a noncommittal gesture, "It comes in handy. Few people cross a man who attires himself with human scalps. Oh, I admit I may have added a few in my time, but only out of necessity."

Zelia breathed a sigh of relief, and Ares fed another stick into the fire.

"We make a great couple. You, abandoned and then fostered by one of Og's rejects, and I . . . I was expelled from the Healers' College for killing a slaver."

His eyes snapped to hers. "A slaver? No great loss, then." He paused. "So, lovely lady, where are you headed?"

"I follow the wind," Zelia said.

"Ah, then you are headed in the right direction. Shall we continue together?"

Zelia took another contemplative bite of dragonpear fruit and chewed it. Mentally, she probed him and met with the same dense, icy fog she had sensed in the past.

His hand went to his forehead. An expression of pain flickered across his face, and he turned to stare at her. "I would really prefer it if you didn't do that. It's not very polite."

She disregarded his statement. "You can shield," she said.

"Of course, there's got to be some advantage to being a half-breed, don't you think?"

Zelia said nothing, musing. He had followed her since Abruzzi, but he had also saved her from . . . what? She thought of last night's battle amongst the stars. She did not know. Besides, his sword had come in handy this morning. Zelia did not share his belief that she would have won this contest unaided.

Better the wolf you know . . . she thought, and inclined her head in assent.

"Yes," Zelia said out loud. "I would be glad of your company."

The Matriarch had to resist the impulse to step away from the raving sheik. His common speech was so garbled that she could scarcely understand a word he said. A large man, he towered above her, but she wouldn't be cowed in her own chambers, so the priestess stood her ground.

The sheik was a handsome man, with his dark hair and flashing black eyes, and the Matriarch understood what there was to turn an elemental's head. His immense size explained, at least in part, Zelia's stature. The Matriarch marvelled that Zelia's mother had managed to carry and bear a child of Zelia's all-too-mortal proportions. It indicated a woman more stalwart and sturdy than most of the airy kind.

"Well?" he said, planting himself in front of her, legs splayed.

Frantically, the Matriarch tried to recall the last thing he had said. She had not expected this reaction, and again she wondered about the wisdom of her message. It seemed a simple act of human generosity at the time – telling him to stop his stipend – but even she had missed the largesse in their coffers.

The man looked at her curiously and seemed to understand. He repeated his sentence for her more slowly and a little bit louder. "You . . . mean . . . to tell me that you have sent my daughter out all alone to battle the sorcerer Queb, and that you have no idea where she is and no way of contacting her unless she chooses to contact you?"

The Matriarch winced. It sounded pretty callous put that way. "That's about the size of it."

"So what do you intend to do about it?"

"Nothing. What can be done has been done, and I send prayers nightly for her protection."

"I'm sure that's a great help," he said sarcastically.

"As I told your daughter, we could not have kept her safe within these walls, not if Queb had decided to find her. We would have put every other cleric in this institution at risk and the patients too, if we had tried to shield her here. Your daughter seemed to understand; it's too bad that you cannot."

"Yes, and my daughter has less sense than her mother. Well, I for one don't intend to sit aside as she goes traipsing off to get herself killed. I will track her and find her, or if not her, then this wizard of which you speak. Either way she can expect a good hiding from me. And if I didn't think I'd find myself in the Hades plane, I'd run you through for exposing her to such danger."

"'Twas not I that created this danger," the Matriarch murmured, and then she swallowed hard. She had said too much already.

WANTED DEAD OR ALIVE . . .

The bounty hunter, Lothair, examined the faded poster and chuckled at the moustache scrawled across the fair features. He recognized his quarry's handiwork. Each poster they had come across along their path had been defaced with the same glib humour.

His partner, Chigbert, returned from where he was scavenging around in the grass. "No doubt about it. They camped here overnight."

The maid had shown some wit by following this back road, sandwiched between mountains and pasture. The track had been difficult to trace, one set of wagon wheels being pretty much like another, but her reputation betrayed her. The news of the couple's passage lingered as the locals talked of the strange blue maid who could cure with a touch, and her snow-white companion.

Lothair nodded and grunted. His brows dipped in frustration over his scarred face. His countenance had once been fair and he stood to be elevated to leader of his tribe. But the youth had contracted the bloody pox, and no man so disfigured can lead others. He tore the weathered picture down, shredding it and tossing the pieces to the winds. He did not want to share this prize with anyone; he had a personal score to settle.

The other watched him, worried. His partner was taking this far too seriously.

Zelia was catapulted from her trance, jolting upright, disorientated and blinking for an instant before the world swam into focus. *Good,* she thought, *we are travelling in the right direction.* His evil influence was spread all across the north, radiating from two points. Soon they would turn east and head towards the Wastes. The call from this circle, warped by Queb so long ago, was strongest. It beckoned to her, and it seemed logical that he would return there.

Tomorrow they would head northeast, away

from the mountains into the gentle rolling hills that eventually flattened to the plains and later the Wastes – Og's home.

Her gaze flicked to Ares. He regarded her with the glinting eyes of the predator, his strange length-wise pupils constricted to a slit. His face was unreadable, but there was something about his expression which bespoke hunger, yearning and greed, and nothing in his demeanour to indicate friendship.

Yet the mercenary was a good man to have at her back in a brawl. She knew that. What Zelia couldn't fathom was what he wanted from her. Clearly he wanted something other than companionship. They argued all the time.

Recalling the Matriarch's counsel, the healer held her peace and remained vigilant whenever Ares was around. The high priestess had said there was one she could trust, but who was to say if this was the one? And there was much to indicate that he was not.

Her gaze fell on the belt of scalps which hung about his waist and she remembered the wraith next to the standing stone. The icy hand of death clutched at her throat. Calming herself with a *pranayama*, Zelia lowered herself to the ground and rolled over to sleep, but sleep was a long time in coming.

* * *

Ares watched Zelia from under the thick veil of his white lashes. He too was pretending to sleep. Neither slumbered, although Ares could tell by the healer's breathing that she had descended into a deep trance and would not awaken if he moved.

He sat up, pupils narrowed to slits as he regarded the radiant blue circle that surrounded her.

Where did she go?

If the mercenary squinted just right, he could see her phantom form reach out and grasp a strand of the wavering ley-line, and then she would soar away, a pulsating, throbbing ripple that shivered up the silvery ley cord, moving swiftly.

The darting blue essence skittered this way and that, and he could tell she searched for something. Whatever it was eluded her, for she flitted aimlessly to and fro, stopping where her control and her spirit form was stretched too thin.

Ares wanted to follow her, but could not. Not in this waking world, only in his sleep when he traversed the Dream Fields. Wide awake, he was earthbound, and the elf-man could only envy her her freedom. Expressions of sorrow, anger and torment flickered across his face, as Zelia sat up, blinking.

Her head swivelled on her neck, and she

peered at him intently. Without a word she reclined, turning over on her side to face away from him as if he didn't exist, but the mercenary noticed that her spine remained rigid and tense for a long time.

The brazen chatter of healer's bells rang out across the dale, and a woman's voice sang a bawdy tune that carried far and wide. Her hair was the colour of the night sky. The wagon she drove was painted in eye-popping colours. Every once in a while, when she stirred on the seat, her dark cloak would open, revealing a crystal tunic that sparkled in the sun. Next to the wagon, a man with shocking white hair rode a great warhorse, but unlike any greybeard the boy had ever known, this one sat straight and proud and his slim face was clean-shaven and unwrinkled. He half-sang, half-shouted the refrain.

The urchin straddled a low hanging branch and watched the spectacle with stunned disbelief. Slipping from his perch, the child ran off in the direction of the village to tell people of their approach.

Zelia's ears pricked at the whisper of the lad's passage, but she did not interrupt her off-key refrain. Her hand strayed to her sword hilt, and her eyes locked with Ares'. When the small figure bolted from behind a tree and dashed screeching around the bend, she breathed a sigh of relief.

With one leg provocatively propped, Zelia settled back in the wagon, in no hurry now. The news of their arrival would precede them. News of her skills, always slightly exaggerated, travelled before them as though borne on the wind, announcing their advance throughout the land from Uri to Norvon.

They had left the road that skirted Eubonia's granite spine and crossed the boundary further to the east. Zelia had to admit she would have been lost without Ares, for she did not know the Norvon tongue. Her Uri was bad at best. She was able to repeat a message with little or no comprehension of its text, but most of the Uri spoke the common speech, and so she had been able to make herself understood. But her Norvon was, if possible, even worse, and here in the hindlands so close to the Wastes, caravans seldom journeyed and only a few spoke common speech.

The wagon jounced around a bend, and the village sprang from nowhere, round huts sprouting like a fairy ring of mushrooms from the same earth of which they were made. Zelia whistled and the mare, grown sleek and fat under her gentle care, began to prance, picking up her dainty hooves in a frolicking gait that contradicted her age. The hen Flighty clasped the bell rope in her beak, as she had been taught, and pulled while Ares began to thump on a drum.

The maid slid out of her cloak, and the crystalline cloth of the modified robes flared under a noonday sun that provided little warmth. The Norvon winter lingered and trees were still bare, without even a hint of the first green of spring. It was so cold Zelia was glad her skin was already blue.

She stood up in the wagon and her robe rippled, dazzling the eye and drawing men and women like flies to dragonpear fruit. With the practice of many rehearsals, she and Ares switched from the bawdy bar-room ditty to another familiar tune, the words of which she had rewritten with a very specific intent and which Ares had translated into barking Norvon.

Come one, come all. Come. I have what you seek.
Just a moment of your time. Come take a peek.
Sachets for love, for protection from foes;
Oil for anointing of fingers and toes;
Amulets and talismans for courage or prowess.
Come hither. Come hither. My wares are the best.

The poetry left a lot to be desired, but the melody was catchy and it served its purpose. Pen and pale soon emptied, and people ran from the fields with shouts of greeting. By the time the wagon finally creaked to a halt, the entire village had gathered.

With a spring in her step, Zelia leapt from her seat. The crystal-laden cloth caught the light and the crowd gasped in awe. Ares dismounted, helping her set up her wares. He dragged clattering cartons from the wagon while she pulled down one of its sides to create a shelf upon which they could display their goods.

Each movement Zelia made was choreographed to enhance the effect of sunlight on tunic and the chattering of small chimes. Thus, unloading appeared a dance. All the while Ares and she continued to sing. Zelia warbled the names of her many wares, hoping that she was pronouncing the unfamiliar Norvon properly, and Ares chanted their price, his deep voice like a drumbeat. Item and price. Item and price.

It had been his idea, something he'd come up with one night when they had had a bit too much *kumys*. It had also been his idea to claim that he had once been a nine-weight weakling, miraculously cured by Og's Rejuvenator. Their sales had increased vastly. She kept a careful eye on him, for there *was* more than a touch of larceny in the lad.

Once everything was ready, she twirled. The slitted side of her garb revealed the soft blue of her flank. The short skirt swirled to show shapely legs. Zelia juggled two of her favourite crystals, then three, four and five, before a rapt audience. Without missing a beat, she explained the virtues of her tonics, using the speech Ares had prepared, and hoping fervently that she wasn't calling the audience dogs or any other such nonsense.

After that Zelia would retreat to station herself next to the display while Ares tumbled, doing back flips and somersaults, and challenged the village youths to a wrestling match. No matter who challenged him, Ares always won by fair means or foul. Then it would be announced that the elf-man had been transformed by Zelia's tonics. Once a man had commented that the adventurer was so pale he looked sick. Ares had given *him* a good trouncing.

If any were unwilling to let go of their markers, the slight tinkle of the enchanted coins Zelia kept within the strongbox soon changed their minds.

Before long, the villagers had formed a queue before the wagon to browse and peruse the sparkling talismans, bottles of oil and many medicants. Zelia continued to parrot their virtues while Ares astounded the reluctant ones with illusionist magic, lest any unwary customer slip away before he had been separated from his cash.

This day an old woman was their first. She approached, held up a clay marker and pointed to a bottle of Universal Specific. Zelia noted the yellowing eyes and peeling skin and quietly refused.

"No, little mother, I have something much better," she said, rummaging around until she found the proper herbs for jaundice. The woman extended a hand with the clay bangles, and Zelia waved it away. She was satisfied with her sales. They had enough to eat tonight and tomorrow and had little need of more.

A second queue had started to form a little way from the first. From her position, Zelia could see a child with the pox and an old man with palsy. She set up a small screen so that she could treat their ills with some privacy. Flighty cackled in protest as two men burst in on them, carrying a man with a gangrenous leg.

One look at the limb, and she grabbed a bottle of Specific, indicating with a swift motion of her hand for the man to drink, and drink deeply. He groaned as Zelia headed for the wagon and silently collected her instruments – the sharp lance and, after a few moments' thought, the saw.

Ares took one look at the saw and withdrew, taking the villagers with him so that they would not be disturbed by the man's screams. With a wince of sympathy Zelia returned to the injured man, urging him to drink more, and when he was suitably soused she began the distasteful task of amputation.

Shouts came to her from somewhere at the far end of the field where the mercenary was teaching the locals the fine art of juggling.

Long, dark fingers bent the tufts of grass to expose the imprint below. *Tracking in this land of rain was child's play,* thought the sheik. He released the blades and they sprang upright again. His long-flowing southron robes whipped about him, and he peered at the trail up ahead. His daughter was making good time, despite her archaic mode of transport. He couldn't understand why she should have given up her fine steed. If speed was important, then the stallion would have helped.

Certainly, secrecy was not important to her. She had left a trail behind her that a blind bounty hunter could follow. Even if the wagon hadn't left a trail a mile wide along this unbeaten path, her passage had hardly gone without comment. Every village talked of the strange blue maid who could swear and drink like a sailor, could fight like a berserker, and whose hands could heal with a touch. His daughter openly thumbed her nose at the authorities, flouted every rule of law or decorum, and came out the heroine. It was so like her.

Only luck could have kept her from the droves of bounty hunters who would have happily traded her scalp for a few markers or a single gold disc. His opinion of the Matriarch's prayers rose considerably, for the sheik had met more than his share of them and had easily dissuaded them from their quest with the promise of twice the coin if they ignored both the poster and the law and returned the girl to him unharmed. All save one was persuaded. This man had respected the authorities – and the girl's reputed sorcery – more than he did the sheik's scimitar. Evidently, here was an *honest* bounty hunter, and Zelia's father was amazed. The man died anyway. The sheik slew him without too much regret. Where his daughter's life was concerned, fidelity to civil authority and honesty were not traits to be admired.

Since he was in unfamiliar terrain, the sheik thought it prudent to hire local mercenaries to help him trace Zelia. It ensured their continued loyalty. Soon, however, it became obvious that she was following a straight course due north. They were two days behind Zelia and her companion. Her father scowled at the thought of her male compatriot. Perhaps a marriage would be in order as soon as the sheik straightened out that other mess his daughter had got herself into back at Pelopnos.

Someone else also trailed her, and who knew their intent? The father doubted that it was friendly. They were only one day behind and would undoubtedly reach her first. It would appear that Zelia's elemental luck had run out.

They traversed the plain outside the Wastes. The wind cut close across the flatlands with a forlorn wail. The trees were little more than thin shrubs that canted towards the south, as if craving its warmth. The vegetation changed the closer they got to the sacred circle, becoming twisted and stunted.

Spring had finally come to the north, and the grass had turned a sullen green. Starflowers bloomed in profusion. Their spiked petals contained a deadly venom which, if distilled, had healing properties, but they did not stop to gather any.

The great circle, at the base of the peninsula that was Szatmar, was visible for miles. Zelia stood awed by its magnitude. During her travels she had seen several of the portals where the ley-lines converged like spokes on a wheel. Her father had taken her to the circle of Shamir where she had been conceived. Both colleges drew their power from the great circle of Thessalia. As a messenger, she had seen the circle which straddled Lavanthia and Shalop. All seemed puny and pale in comparison with this gargantuan structure. The stones were burnt and scorched, their tops broken off in several places.

Few truly understood the circles. The wizards knew them to be the places where the many lines in the grid converged, and used their magic accordingly. Some believed the circles were giant temples built by the gods to mark the doors, while others said that they were the last frozen remnants of the earth elementals, ancestors to the trolls, who had been caught in the doorways when they closed to man. But no one debated their ultimate purpose; *all* agreed that they housed the doors that separated the planes. This one was reputed to be the doorway to the Brimstone plane, fire's realm, and Zelia could well believe it, for it was warmer here than elsewhere in this barren land, and the earth around them was dried and cracked.

Stirred by memory, Ares walked up and stroked the lichen-encrusted rock. He made a movement as if to march between the stones, but Zelia stopped him with a dissonant clanking of bells.

"Don't! 'Tis fatal for mortal man to enter the portals."

Ares glanced up at the huge frowning monolith beside him. "Is it? I seem to remember being surrounded on all four sides by jagged stones. It was a strange sensation looking up at the sky, very much like sitting in the mouth of some great dragon."

"Perhaps you were protected by your blood. *I* would never try it," Zelia said. "You can go through if you want to. Who knows where you'll end up? But you couldn't pay me enough to step between those stones."

"What? Leave you and miss all this?" he quipped, gesturing at the brown wasteland.

"Well, yes," Zelia sagged against the stone. "It would appear I've led us on a wild goose chase."

Ares gave her a sidelong glance. "Perhaps I could help you if you told me what you seek," he said slyly.

She ignored him.

"Let's get out of here," Zelia said, climbing back into the wagon. "That is, if you've finished traipsing down memory lane. There's nothing here, not even punters to buy physick."

"I told you so," Ares grumbled under his breath, adding, "I wish I knew what you were looking for."

He groused continually as he remounted. Zelia turned the wagon to face the east, clucking and muttering at the reluctant Heifer. Her bells chattered at each bump and fissure in the barren soil.

"Can't you keep those things quiet? They're giving me a headache." Ares swung his mount around. "Come on you, poor dumb beast – back the way we came."

She whispered the appropriate spell before snapping back at him, "Why don't you name that animal? It's got spirit. It's got pride. It deserves a name."

"He," Ares corrected.

"He," she said.

"You don't name what you may have to eat some day."

Zelia's mouth clapped shut and her desert blood boiled. In Shamir, horses were everything. Their milk fed the babe or was fermented for the adult to imbibe. They were the medium of exchange. Their quality and their lines betokened a man's wealth and esteem. A sheik was a sheik because his horses won the great annual race, thus each sheik must always breed the best to maintain his title. Yet looking at this lifeless barren plain, she could not argue the point. What would they eat if they didn't have the wagon for provisions? It was a depressing thought.

The air around them was oppressively hot and muggy, and Zelia longed to be far from the circle's radiating warmth. Every once in a while she stole a sideways glance at her companion. What manner of man was this who had been found outside such a place? Who had walked within a sacred circle and survived?

Ares set a hurried pace, and soon they were back on the narrow isthmus of land between the Wastes and the mountains that formed the border between Norvon and Szatmar. This place was the crossroads. The main road travelled north and south, and there was a straggling pass that was the only route over the mountains to the far western kingdom of Firth. An inn had been built at the juncture. They arrived at the lonely establishment a little after sunset.

Frozen to the bone, Ares and Zelia huddled together, savouring each other's warmth. A small fire hiccuped dirty clouds of smoke in their faces where they sat on a hard wooden bench next to the hearth. The surly innkeeper plunked bowls of lumpy stew on the scarred table before them and Zelia looked up, surprised at his manner. This place was not so close to civilization that it could afford to lose custom, any custom. Ares bent forward and scraped crusted food from the table's surface with his knife.

The huffing innkeeper noted Zelia's bemused expression and remarked, abruptly. "We don't like your kind here," gesturing towards their weapons and the belt of scalps around Ares' waist. Too tired to squabble, Zelia took a spoonful of the unpalatable mixture and swallowed it reluctantly as the innkeeper backed away.

Ares raised his dagger to point at him. "My friend and I would like a room."

"We're full up."

Zelia gaped. They gazed at the empty room, and their eyes locked. Ares rose menacingly, the knife still in his hand.

The landlord scurried behind his bar and fidgeted amongst his belongings. Extracting a book, he flipped nervously through the pages. "I see here that we have one, er, vacancy. Just one, mind you. You'll have to share."

Sinking to his seat, Ares draped an arm around Zelia. "That would be just fine," he said.

The maid of summer blue moaned, shook his arm off and sidled away from him.

* * *

The wind howled in the eaves and ruffled the thatch on the stable roof. The innkeeper hopped from foot to foot and rubbed his arms briskly, trying to keep warm. His face was flushed with exertion by the time two huge shadows separated from the darkness and slid silently towards him.

"Your, ah, friends are abed in a room in the back. The last time I passed all was quiet. I think they are sleeping," the innkeeper said. He opened his mouth to speak again, knowing that he was blathering to cover his anxiety, for he liked the look of these bounty hunters less than the two inside, despite their dubious parentage. These two looked half-troll, but their markers were good enough, he supposed.

The first man interrupted him. "Did the woman carry anything of magic? Any wands? Any amulets? She's a powerful sorceress."

"None beside the junk they tried to sell me." The fat brow furrowed. "At least, nothing that I saw. Hey, she's not gonna burn my place down, is she?"

"Not if you keep mum," the first man reassured the innkeeper as he handed him a gold coin. "Come," he said to the second. "Let us join our *friends*."

The innkeeper didn't wait until they had

dismissed him. He scampered off, the coin clenched to his breast.

As they moved away, Chigbert spoke to his companion. "I told you you shouldn't have given that fat slob a disk. A bronze or a copper marker would have done."

"Don't worry, he won't keep it." Lothair made a quick slicing motion with his finger across his throat. "But there's no point letting this fellow get cold feet. This way we've ensured he'll stay quiet. I don't know about you, but I don't relish the idea of spending the rest of my life as a pig like that young apprentice we heard tell about in Thessalia."

Lothair unsheathed his blade. "We'll get the coin back when we're through with our business here."

The wizard drooped limply against the wall of the cavern. The pentagram flickered brightly on the floor, faded and went out. His body grew weak and he could no longer raise the demon that had told him of the half-breed's approach, although any Devil's imp was balky and uncooperative at the best of times. Still, Queb could sense her movement almost as soon as she left the circle, as if she had picked up something of its magic.

The necromancer levered himself away from

the wall and hobbled across the cave to the bubbling cauldron. He sniffed at the mixture, grimaced and lifted it to his lips. He must build up his strength before her arrival.

CHAPTER 8

Something soft covered her face and Zelia could not breathe. She flailed blindly. Her questing fingers found flesh, and she clawed at the unseen assailant. Pandemonium broke out all around her.

Her fingers touched something wet. *An eye!* As she raked her hand downwards, an agonized shriek came from the blank space above her head and the pressure on the cloak or coverlet, or whatever it was that her attacker held over her face, slackened.

Zelia struggled free of the entangling cloth, thrusting it from her. She rolled off the pallet on to her hands and knees and panted desperately.

Air rasped into burning lungs and she tried to remember where she'd left her sword.

In the centre of the room, Ares fought for his life. His hammer cut a broad swathe before him and his dagger flittered like lightning in the darkened room, but he was losing ground. His opponent was a red-haired behemoth with a pockmarked face who seemed to know him, for between jabs, he called the adventurer by name.

Before she had a chance to assimilate this information, the firemaker's wand appeared in her hands. Zelia stared at it stupidly for a moment. *It rarely came even if she called*. Then realization dawned on her face, and she motioned for Ares to make his way towards the door. He caught her frenzied gestures, nodded, and gathered his legs for a leap over his adversary. The hammer arced and connected with one man's skull with a sickening crack. Ares sprang. Zelia scooped up her sword and cloak and followed. When they had reached the door, she paused, letting rip, and the room burst into flames. Ares raced ahead of her and the fire lapped eagerly at her heels.

Outside, their stride faltered. They halted, briefly and Ares turned to stare at her handiwork. He chuckled softly, "And another inn bites the dust!"

* * *

Dawn found them west, heading towards the mountain pass to Firth. They had quarrelled all morning. Zelia's nerves were raw and on edge. She did not trust any man whose friends attacked them in the middle of the night. Ares silenced her, saying that they were no friends of his, but competitors. This did little to ease Zelia's troubled mind and their conversation had long since drifted down the querulously tortured paths of regular contention, shifting from this grievance to that.

She countered, her exasperation apparent in her tones. "If my maps are correct, there's a plateau beyond that mount. That's the principality of Merovnick. We should find people there."

"About time! This place is as still as Death's planes," Ares said. It was a familiar complaint. "We haven't made a single clay marker since *you* decided to take us to the Wastes."

The scent of overripe fruit and dried herbs surrounded her. The wagon had fallen into happy disarray. Herbs dangled from the rafters. Magical paraphernalia rolled around on the floor, wound in scrolls and tangling with scraps of blood-stained cloth. Food-caked platters and crusted pots bounced along with apple cores and bits of mouldy black bread.

"You could have left any time," she snarled,

although she didn't mean it. He was a good man in a fight. His sturdy arm had saved her from the bounty hunters – bounty hunters who had called him by name – and she noted cynically that he had been saving his own hide also.

The firemaker's wand stirred inside her tunic, where it had hidden itself, perhaps picking up her agitation. It must have learned to like her. Since the incident at the inn, it had secreted itself on her person. Twice she had tried to put it away, then she would shift on the wagon seat and find the crystal wand stabbing her in the back, breast or thigh. Finally Zelia gave up, pocketing it comfortably in her jerkin when she arose each morning.

It purred against her skin, and Zelia felt a warmth growing inside her as the image of Ares, arms slick with sweat, standing with his war hammer in his hands, rose in her mind.

Why the scheming little matchmaker! she thought. But Zelia felt an odd sense of kinship with the man – two half-breeds, two misfits, two renegades of church and craft loosed upon the world.

"All I said," Ares interjected, "was we'd make more money if you charged more for your treatment. With the population being so sparse, we could use the extra funds."

"And all *I* suggested was," Zelia countered, "if you wouldn't mind relinquishing your manhood without benefit of anaesthesia, you might make a good healer."

They quibbled back and forth, with the thrust and parry of verbal assault, as they always did, and Ares swore up and down that he would leave her, as he often did.

"You are stubborn and headstrong," he said. The wand peeked out of her pocket. "Everything a woman isn't supposed to be. And I wish you'd put that wand away. One of these days you're going to get us burned as heretics!"

Ares' stallion scrabbled in the loose scree, performing a bumping slide into the wagon, and his argument lost some of its dignity. His mouth snapped shut and he spurred his mount ahead. They concentrated on the trail before them in leaden silence.

The narrow track wound along a slope of slippery gravel that ended fifty metres below in a sheer cliff. The footing was precarious, and the gentle hill to either side deceptively seductive.

A rocky overhang some one hundred metres ahead heralded the end of the loose scrabble and rough pebbles of the slide area. There the track narrowed, leaving only enough room for a single wagon.

The sun had begun its nightly retreat and an early mist gathered, rolling slowly up from the gorge. It crept silently like a young cutpurse intent on his victim, reeking of decay. Something about the encroaching fog seemed deadly.

Ares stopped and Zelia cast an uneasy glance at her partner. He gazed down at the amorphous white wall with mild distaste and concern. It wouldn't be long before it overtook them. With the precipice directly to their right and the smooth wall of slate soaring skyward on their left, a single misstep would send her and her cart plummeting over the edge of the cliff. The horses plodded forward, oblivious to all danger.

Gossamer tendrils sent grasping fingers swirling around them. The straggly mountain vegetation dripped monotonously, and the mist muted all sound; even Zelia's ringing bells grew dull and sodden. They moved in single file with Ares in the lead, and Zelia could barely see the rump of his great destrier. Her mare stumbled and the healer swore. The mist absorbed her voice, devouring it.

A deep recess appeared in the rock wall to her left. She reined in Heifer and called ahead before clambering from her seat. Ares pivoted in his saddle. She pointed to the craggy overhang and handed him her reins. Pulling her sword from its scabbard and the firemaker's wand from her pocket, she moved towards the cave.

At its mouth she crouched, pausing to summon firemaker's light from the pure essence of the fiery creatures contained within the wand. Glowing with the brilliance of two moons, the orb danced gaily on the wand's tip, and Zelia urged it forward with a brisk wave. The pulsating ball bounced away, skittering ahead to illuminate the cave's interior. She crept cautiously after it, her eyes darting around the small alcove, looking for sign of previous habitation. She came across some bleached bones, twigs and the scattered remains of a long-dead fire.

Zelia turned to call Ares, only to discover him standing behind her, battle hammer in hand. She jumped, almost losing her footing and falling into his arms. He grimaced an apology. Zelia turned and sent the light to hover at the back of the cave. A small hole in the far wall indicated an interconnecting corridor. They both frowned as she nudged the light into the tiny orifice.

Ares got down on his hands and knees and looked in. "I don't like it," his voice echoed in the hollow tunnel. The adventurer straightened. "It's not a good set-up."

"I admit it's not ideal, but I don't like the look of that fog, and I don't think we're going to find much better up ahead." Zelia looked from him to the roiling mist at the cave's mouth.

"Not to mention the risk of falling over the cliff," he said. "I suppose I'd rather spend the night guarding our backs, but it's not much of a choice."

"Look on the bright side," she said as she stooped to peer into the bore. "It's not big enough to house much more than an anorectic wraith."

Ares looked at her, his lips pursed, but he withheld any comment. She stood up to fetch Heifer, who was happily nibbling on scrub next to the path. Flighty clucked as the mare stripped a knobbly twig and belched. Zelia unhitched her from the wagon, plucked the hen from its perch and took them both into the cave. She paused briefly to brush down the horses as Ares stacked the wood for their fire alongside the long-unused hearth.

He grumbled over flint and iron, whispering oaths that would have turned the skin of an Ogress lily white, but the tinder resisted all human means of igniting. Impatiently Zelia zapped it with the firemaker's wand. Ares leapt out of harm's way with a sharp screech of complaint. The force of the blow set the rocks to glowing and warmed the entire chamber immediately. Ares' hair steamed.

"Oops! Sorry." As a peace-making gesture, she said, "I'll take first watch."

Zelia fiddled with the feeble flames, trying to find something, anything, to keep herself awake. She whipped the coals into a frenzy. Then she formed letters, runes, or fantastical images. Sometimes serpentine creatures stared blandly back at her. Even as she watched, a salamander blinked, yawned and then dissipated in flames.

The healer longed to sleep. The odious mist had seeped into the cave itself, where it billowed in a blood-red cloud, reflecting the fire's light. The sulphurous fumes clung to her, and she wondered if she'd ever be able to wash the stench out of her hair. Her mind wandered to the innocuous hole towards the rear of the cave. She saw no real danger there, but resolved to stay alert, and with that thought, she drifted into a fitful slumber.

The Lady Astra reclined listlessly on the stony ledge of the fountain, in a rare moment of calm. Her hand dangled dolefully into the pond. She gave up. Whatever it was, it was well and truly lost. Gone. She didn't have it. She couldn't find it, and she wasn't even sure what it was.

Her watery cousins sang comfort. The elemental smiled wanly and peered into the pool's depths. Her reflection and that of the stones behind her blurred. With a look of concentration unusual for one of her kind, the Lady summoned the image of her daughter. She slept, wrapped in a dark cloak, next to a handsome young man. The glowing fire simpered and died, and mist swirled around a rocky cavern. The lady nodded her approval of the young man.

A misshapen shadow loomed over the sleeping couple, and the Lady Astra shrieked a warning across the planes. The water elementals faltered in their endless ebb and flow. Even the fire ceased its capering for a moment, and Earth humphed with cumbersome slowness. Then life resumed once more.

Chapter 9

A distant sound woke her from her light doze. She gestured at the fire and a spiralling shower of sparks lit the entire cavern. Then the fire darkened, spent by the bright display, but not before she saw a furtive movement near the small mouth of the bore. With a sharp inhalation, she rose to her feet. But before she was fully erect, Zelia felt warty hands cover her mouth, pulling her off balance. She whispered the words of a spell into a clammy palm, but before she could complete it, Zelia felt a sharp, blinding pain behind her left ear, and all went black.

She came to, face down, cheek pressed against

wet stone. Water dripped . . . somewhere. She was bound hand and foot, her limbs completely immobilized. A single guttering torch lit what must have been a rocky corridor far beyond their cave.

Harsh voices clashed above her head in a hissing, sibilant speech difficult to understand. It was a guttural form of common speech, spoken in such way that it sounded obscene. Clearly, they were arguing over her, like soldiers over prized booty. It took little imagination to figure what they had in mind. Zelia forced both mind and body to relax while she tried to concentrate on what her captors said.

Someone stepped between her and the torch. The sickly yellow light threw a frighteningly misshapen shadow across the floor. Not one, but *two* pairs of long arms dangled from a bent and deformed back. Its knuckles scraped against the floor. A tail swept into her line of vision. A hand poked her ribs and stroked her hip, and slimy fingers ran over her flank to her thigh.

"Yes-s-s, our mas-s-ter will be pleaz-z-ed. This-s-s one will breed well. S-she iz-z-z s-sturdy. Perhaps-s-s-s he will reward me for s-s-such a priz-ze." Suddenly the words formed by the sibilant syllables started to make sense. Zelia quivered involuntarily.

"Get up, pries-s-stess-s-s-s-s!" The creature made the word sound like an accusation rather than a term of respect. "Get up! We know you are awake. We will not carry you."

Zelia struggled to sit up. She felt rough hands reach down and cut her bonds, and she rose to stare at the *thing* that spoke to her. Two pink-tinged eyes glared from a glistening distorted visage, a thing of nightmare, with no nose and strange lumps where there should be none. She gulped convulsively and looked around.

A party of twenty-five assorted creatures surrounded her, no two alike. They regarded her warily, a few from a single eye planted in the middle of a wrinkled forehead, some from two eyes, others from three. Many were covered in matted fur, others were hairless, while still others showed the scales of a reptile. On one, she counted no less than four pairs of arms. Their ugly features made their expressions difficult to decipher, but there was no mistaking the speaker's attitude. He drooled as he looked at her. Whether he was thinking of a tenday joint, or an unwedded bride, Zelia didn't know and she didn't want to find out.

The commander wore a cloak over a shirt of chain mail modified to accept both pairs of arms. The creature was barrel-chested, with talons curling from both sets of hands and feet.

The beast shoved her rudely down the dark corridor. "Get moving!"

Zelia moved, shaking her head to clear it with the sweet chatter of chimes. The captain cuffed her. "Sssshut up! The clatter izzz enough to wake the dead!"

Her temper flared briefly as she whispered a silencing spell, but the output of power caused the tunnel to swirl about her giddily. Zelia realized that she felt sluggish as if she had been . . . drugged. *Of course, the mists. The fog was poisoned. Or drugged!*

That's why she had fallen asleep, despite her best efforts. She wondered what had become of her companion. Poor Ares was probably dead or, if he was lucky, out cold. Who knew if he would wake tomorrow from the toxic mist? If his elfin luck held, then his skull would be intact and whole, not crushed by some creature's mace. Any residual effects of the drug dispersed with that thought, and Zelia began to look about her in earnest, searching for an exit. The group clattered along a narrow hall, and her heart sank. The walls were smooth without a single branch or adjoining tunnels in sight.

The mutants joked among themselves, congratulating each other on their catch. A priestess, a priestess of the accursed Brigitta. They would be rewarded, perhaps with her remains.

They spoke with reverence of their unnamed master, and Zelia's blood ran cold. Escape seemed impossible. Even if she managed it, she wondered if she would be able to find her way back to their small cave.

How long had she been unconscious, and how far had she been carried?

The corridor ended abruptly in steep stairs. She peered over the shoulder of the creature in front of her to get a good look at the steps. They were, she conceded, of fine workmanship – even, smooth, with regularly spaced risers. This place had not been formed by human hands. At least Zelia would not need to worry about tripping as she went into a trance. She let her legs carry her as she centred psychically, concentrating on the rhythm of the movement, the regular stretch and contraction of muscles in calf and thigh. She let the rhythm soothe her until she had achieved a meditative state.

Then she mentally cast about her, following the corridor back, still able to read the group's collective aura in the breathless air. It glowed most strongly where they had halted and argued, but from there it grew fainter until it died completely. By then, however, she could sense another, gentler, gleam of white.

He lived! She attempted to touch Ares' mind, and for once met no resistance. She found herself churning with wrath and throbbing pain. With a shock, the maid realized she could see the dark sloping corridors swim swiftly beside her, and Zelia knew she looked through his eyes. *He followed!*

Quickly Zelia withdrew, pulling back into herself, and her eyes popped open. He lived, and he followed! There was hope yet. Breathing a sigh of relief, she studied the long line of raiders before her. An equal number trailed behind. She'd give them something to think about! Zelia, daughter of Sheik Al Y Kazzam, would not be taken quietly, like some terem bride. She'd let them know that she was no common cleric, humble and compliant.

Slowly Zelia began to tease the torch flame, calling a wind to tickle it into a bright flare. The beasts recoiled from its brilliant intensity. The leader, who walked directly behind her, kicked her in the kidneys. She staggered, whipping around to glare at the bloodshot eyes.

"Quit it, witch woman!"

Zelia acquiesced belligerently, sending the flame leaping towards the roof in a final pyrotechnic display.

"Very pretty. Will you do s-such things-s-s to entertain our massster?" The leader's snout touched her ear, and she shrank from his foul breath. He sniggered wickedly.

So much for tricks, she thought. But no, she would not give up!

Next, Zelia threw a bafflement spell towards the head of the group. One creature halted, a look of confusion on its monstrous face. The others walked into it. An axe clanged down the stairs. A bony fist reached out and slapped her. Her head rebounded off the smooth wall, and her ears rang.

"Enough!" the commander bellowed. "Any more tricks-s and you'll be out cold. I don't want to damage the merchandis-s-se, but . . ." He let his threat dangle tauntingly before her and then propelled her roughly down the stairs. They marched on, again in an orderly column.

Zelia lost track of time. It seemed as if they had travelled for hours when the stairs finally opened into a broad hall. From this main corridor, many others branched to either side. They continued forward until they reached a door to a narrow stone balcony overlooking a vast subterranean cavern.

Cool mist swirled in billowing clouds, and Zelia tried not to breathe, soon giving up the effort as futile and impractical. They wouldn't poison themselves and their prize chattel, would they? She tried to pierce the gloom and was dismayed by what she saw. The chamber was large enough to house a small city, and did. Strange creatures moved from one level to another. *Thousands of them! An entire settlement!*

The raiding party moved to another set of stairs which snaked along the outer wall to the cavern below. From this vantage point, she could see that many mountain-fed springs kept the air continually moist. Accumulated slate and shale, worn from the walls by the running water, made marshy beds which maintained the sodden environment.

The captain nudged her with his mace, and she turned just in time to see his eyes bulge out as the tip of an arrow miraculously sprouted from his ribcage. Frantically Zelia searched the overhang for Ares and found him. He had already let another bolt fly, catching the leader's servant in the throat. He grabbed a third arrow, nocked it and shot, and a third creature dropped where it stood.

She kicked the first two bodies over the edge of the stairs. They fell to the wet sand below with a dull thud, which was followed by a cry of delight as one of the local inhabitants discovered food apparently dropping from heaven like dinner on a stick. Zelia sent the third body rolling down the steps. It hit the next in line, who had only now begun to react to the commotion. He staggered under the dead weight, falling on top of the creature behind him.

The raiding party below her tumbled like Fennec's sacred cubes. When she turned to look up again, she found that two more had been felled by Ares. She inhaled sharply, sent goddess-blessings to her companion, and began clambering over the fallen corpses. Only nine remained, and without their leader, they scattered in confusion.

The more obstinate ones searched for their opponent and found him, his white hair shining like a beacon in the gloom. With a yell, four separated from the rest and charged towards the stone overhang. Zelia climbed over the fourth body, stopping to heave it over the side to the subterranean swamp below. With a hurried glance over her shoulder, she saw the creatures fighting over the bodies of their fallen comrades. She felt ill.

Another toppled conveniently before her, an arrowhead protruding from its shoulder. She dodged, letting it roll past her. With their comrades neatly dismembered and apportioned, the soldiers on the lower level of stairs resolved to pursue her. Another went down, and Zelia decided this was a good time to beat a hasty retreat. She pivoted and was confronted by the gruesome beast, who had reasoned – rightly enough – that the safest place was at the bottom of the stairs. It brushed past her, ignoring her completely in its rush to escape, but the last soldier was not so obliging. Enraged, it lunged at her, arcing with surprising grace through the air. Ares' arrows caught it mid-leap, and she dodged it as it went crashing head over heels down the stairs.

So far she had been lucky, but she couldn't depend on luck – or Ares' archery – for ever. She saw a gap in the wall and ducked into a place of concealment. There was a yell as Ares realized she was missing, but Zelia had no time to reassure him before she walked right into the arms of the fallen commander. He leaned against the wall, the arrow flopping uselessly from his breast plate.

The creature barked an order and two guards stepped into view. They herded Zelia down a short corridor and then stopped at a door. The commander opened it and waved two arms in unison, in an expansive gesture of invitation.

"Here, priestessss, we have come." And he nudged her through with his mace. "I hope you enjoy your ssstay."

The wounded captain and two guards twittered as they slammed the door shut behind her. Darkness enveloped the healer. It was pitch black, and not even her magically enhanced night vision allowed her to penetrate the gloom. This was no natural shadow; it had to be a spell.

A voice, which sounded like a thousand snakes slithering over sand and a thousand spiders skittering over glass, spoke from behind the shadowy veil that surrounded her.

"Welcome," it said. "I've been expecting you."

Light exploded in front of her and Zelia stared into the face revealed in Brigitta's sacred pond. The wizard was dressed in the black robes of a necromancer, and the symbols embroidered in blood red on his gown were those of ill-omen. The deep cowl did not quite hide the reptilian features or the cadaverous face, the skin covered in scabrous sores. His hand was alight. The fingertips flickered, becoming one with the flame.

'Twas true what they said. He had conquered the Brimstone plane.

The sorcerer motioned about the cavern, and several torches sprang to life. An enormous arachnid shadow jigged along the wall in the frenzied light. Zelia examined the laboratory inquisitively. Cages lined the walls and small, unnamable animals cringed in each. She could only guess at what they had been before, but they had been altered until they were something profane. A legless weasel with the head of an owl slithered like a snake up a bare branch.

Around her were tables whose tops were cluttered with bottles and jars in which floated human parts. Zelia stared in revulsion as the man-sized spider crawled lazily across the ceiling above her head. Then she turned to look at a thick, green mixture that burbled over single flame. It gave a bilious burp and a small yellowish cloud formed above it, spreading noxious fumes.

The wizard followed her gaze, grinned, and pointed a gnarled finger at the viscous fluid. "You like that? This lovely invention will, in turns to come, poison the entire universe. You had a brief introduction to it along the trail. I call it pollution." He shook his hand out and yawned as if bored.

"I suppose I should introduce myself," the necromancer said. "I am Queb, but you've probably already guessed that, haven't you? I am the one you were sent to find."

Zelia recoiled. He had been expecting her! Until this moment, she hadn't really believed that he still lived. Oh, she had believed after a fashion. The Matriarch had said it was true, and she was leader of their craft, so it must be. But the maiden hadn't *really* believed!

Now that Zelia stared into his rheumy eyes, she wondered if she were up to this task. Back at the college, it had all seemed so easy. Like a game or a prank she would have pulled as a child. She'd sneak in and grab his staff under a spell of invisibility. *Hah!* Despair closed in around her. What good was her magic now? What there was of it. What did she know? A few paltry spells of invisibility, of forgetfulness or befuddlement. Enough to dupe a mere mortal or stupid beasts, but not Queb. It suddenly dawned on Zelia that she faced the stuff of legends. He could marshal powers worse than her darkest imaginings. He could summon creatures from the Planes of Death. She cringed, half-expecting some demon, devil or blood-sucking wampyr to materialize before her eyes.

Queb interrupted her thoughts. "You have, no doubt, heard that I was dead, or at least wished it. But as you see, I am alive. Not well, mind you, but alive. Unfortunately, I am weakened by this body in which my spirit dwells." He plucked at the loose flesh that hung from his arms. "I need another, more hospitable shell. Humanity is too weak and puny to be useful. Therefore, I have tried to create what I need, and my creatures are sturdy but unlovely.

"You have already met my friends – failed experiments. They repel and repulse all who see them. But you . . . you are pretty indeed and will suit my purposes nicely. Your talent is untrained, to be sure, and feeble, but I have the skill I need, if not the strength. Still, I will need your powers for the final spell that will free me from this." Queb tapped his bony chest. "And perhaps your body, with its tinge of fey magic, will be stronger than most and can survive this raging spirit."

His breath burned like molten rock inside his lungs, and his head ached as he raced along the corridors. Ares whispered a small prayer of thanks to the god Og for his one-time master, who had done so much to thicken his skull. Many would not have survived such a blow.

The adventurer rushed down blind halls following instinct, as if – through some whiff of her magic – he could sense Zelia's previous passage. Every mercenary's instinct screamed out for him to begone from this dark cave. Yet he followed, probably to his doom. He had need of her, her powers and her skills. Besides, Ares had grown used to her, grouchy and irascible as she was, for the woman accepted him for what he was.

Hearing the clop of nailed feet, Ares retreated into a shadowy alcove. Light flared and he pressed himself against the wall, trying to become part of it. He hit something, and the stones beneath his feet started to move with a harsh grating noise.

He was thrown forward as the earth gave way beneath him and he tumbled into an abyss. A few moments later, he landed on something hard and started to roll, picking up momentum. Rubble and loose dirt followed in his sliding wake. He extended his legs to break his fall and felt them crack against a boulder. After that he curled into a ball, unable to resist the spinning descent.

He was sure he must have hit every rock in the belly of the mountains before he plummeted into gut-wrenching space, only to land with an "oomph!" a short distance later.

Something grated overhead, and Zelia looked up just as Ares dropped like a lead weight to land on the floor beside her. Queb considered him thoughtfully while a miniature gryphon shrieked a vile oath. Zelia whispered the counterspell, but not soon enough, and Ares slid into unconsciousness.

"Naughty, dear," the necromancer admonished, and the next minute, Zelia's lips were bound by a gag spell and her retort came out as a puling peep.

The sorcerer shuffled around a table to inspect Ares.

"Another half-breed. Yes, this one will suit nicely, and you. Well, perhaps I won't be needing your body, after all. Who would want to be shackled with a woman's body?" The wizard hobbled around them, rubbing his chin. "Yes, most unexpected indeed, but you won't give me any trouble, will you? Now that you can save your pretty hide." Queb stooped, stared deep into Zelia's eyes and she was paralysed. He smiled, placed the oozing stump which had once been a hand upon her cheek and stroked it, sloughing a trail of dead skin and slime.

Zelia gulped back the bile that threatened to choke her.

"You would have made quite an apt pupil, but that was not to be. Still, your powers will enhance mine, and your friend will provide a suitable domicile. Much better even than you." With a shrug, the wizard leaned over an open spellbook to study its pages, his back to her. Released from his stare, Zelia felt for the wand, but with the wilful perversity of magical objects, it chose that moment to absent itself from her person.

She groped down Ares' leg until she found the dagger he kept hidden in his boot. Then she threw it. Before the knife had reached its target, the wand materialized out of thin air and she seized it before it could change its mind. It quivered in her hand, tingling with excitement and terror. Zelia hurled a leaping ball of flame. It flew from the wand's tip as the dagger sliced neatly through the thick robes and disappeared into the withered flesh. Little blood oozed from the hole, as if the archmage were so old that he'd grown dry and powdery. Then, as the knife wormed its way to his evil heart, blood as thick as tar erupted in a fountainous spew that doused the fireball.

The flame flickered and dimmed, shrinking to the size of her fist. The enfeebled fireball penetrated the folds of cloth only to be swallowed by the wound and extinguished. Brandishing the wand before her, Zelia was about to create another when the necromancer – exploded!

Queb welcomed the loosening of his body's hold on his spirit. He was only dimly aware of the bits of himself that showered gently over the maid and the unconscious man. He felt the demons of pestilence and plague as they were released from the infirm flesh that had housed them so long. They whisked around the cave for a moment and were gone, and Queb was not sorry to see them go.

Zelia flung herself protectively over Ares, covering her head with her hands, and waited for the splattering of gore she knew must follow. The gag enchantment was lifted, unlocking both tongue and vocal chords, and Ares came to life beneath her.

"You can let me up now," he murmured, but with his face lodged between her breasts, it sounded more like: "Urkoonlefmpner."

The healer levered her body off her companion and looked around, stunned. No blood dripped from the ceiling nor did viscera glide down the wall, rather a fine black powder settled about her shoulders. She covered her nose and mouth with her hand, noting the scorched place on the floor which marked the spot where Queb had once stood.

Ares coughed and gagged and grabbed her hand to pull her up behind him. He made a dash for the door, dragging the dazed Zelia along as he went. She followed unquestioningly. He steered her down the corridor, urging her onward. The encounter had drained her, and she had no will of her own left. She ran because he ran, tracking him through tunnel after tunnel and turn after turn through the dark maze, too stupefied to care whither he led her. Not even survival mattered any more. She ran by reflex, mechanically putting one foot in front of the other. The slap of their footfalls beat a tattoo inside her head that said: *It was too easy, too easy, too easy, too . . .*

Ares skidded to a stop, and Zelia slid into him, nearly knocking him down.

"Ssh!" he put one finger over his mouth while

he pointed ahead. "Look." And Zelia saw a faint pinprick of light, like a star in the night, glittering in the distance.

"Where do you think we are?" she whispered harshly.

"I don't know. We're probably further along the trail than we were last night . . . I hope."

They crept the last few hundred paces. Pausing for a moment to let his eyes adjust to the light, Ares crawled into the early morning sun. All vestiges of last night's mist were gone. Laughing with relief, he turned and helped her slither through the small opening.

"You wait here," he said. "I think I know where we are. I'll go and get the horses – assuming they're not simmering in a stewpot somewhere." And he disappeared into the brush.

A paltry sun played with dust motes raised by his departure, and Zelia's thoughts turned inward. Something was wrong. She could feel it in her bones. Something she had forgotten. She reviewed those last moments: the dagger, the disappearing ball of flame . . . *It was too easy.* He had turned his back on her, leaving her hands free. Such reckless behaviour didn't fit into her image of an all-powerful wizard.

And then there was Ares. He had come after her when he could have saved himself. The

Matriarch had said that there was one she could trust. Could Ares be her unknown helpmate? But Zelia had a hard time reconciling this concept with the stony-eyed stare she had so often noted when he thought he regarded her unaware. Numb from exhaustion, too numb even to think, the healer curled up into a foetal position to await his return.

The clatter of Heifer's halter and the rattle of the wheels roused her from her lethargy. Ares' destrier was tied to the rear of the wagon. The adventurer helped her up into the seat and coaxed Heifer to a trot, wanting to put as much distance as possible between them and the subterranean city. Zelia slouched low in the seat next to Ares. Her eyes were two bruised semicircles, dark as the purple moon, and her brow wrinkled in brooding meditation.

Ares looked over at her uncomfortably. In their time together, he had become all too well acquainted with his unpredictable partner's many moods. She was scheming something, he was sure of it, and he didn't think it was a recipe for a new love potion. They jostled around another bend, the wagon skittering sideways, and Ares glanced over his shoulder, glad to see the mountain top shrinking behind them.

They passed a deserted settlement on the outskirts of the Principality of Merovnick. Zelia snapped her fingers and climbed through the small aperture which led into the wagon's interior, then reappeared rump-first with a scroll clenched in her first. Ares clicked his tongue, trying to persuade the mare to move faster. He didn't like Zelia's expression as she pored over the parchment and obscure runes that he could neither read nor decipher. The wagon teetered precariously as Heifer lurched forward, and the hen pecked at the back of Ares' neck in protest at the bumpy ride. The elfman contemplated for the umpteenth time what a tasty meal the bird would make.

Twisting again, Zelia squirmed through the small window back into the wagon. Something crashed inside, and she popped from the opening – her body sprawled half-in and half-out of the wagon – to snatch the reins from his hands and jerk Heifer to a halt.

"We've got to go back. I forgot his staff."

"What!" he demanded furiously.

"We've got to go back." She shook the scroll at him. "It was too easy."

"Easy? You're nuts!" Ares said as he tried to wrest the reins from her grasp. "We're lucky to be alive and you want to go back!"

Zelia wriggled on to the seat. "Don't you realize that that was Queb? *The* Queb. Not some fly-by-night imitation."

"Queb? Alive after all this time?" Ares said. "Well, if it is, then he's not any more." He gave her a sidelong look. "You killed him, didn't you?"

"No. I mean, yes. I mean, I don't know. Look, this sorcery drains its user of energy, so a wizard is only as strong as his physical body. I may have played right into his hands. He said something about . . ." She grabbed Ares and peered deep into his eyes. His pupils contracted in surprise.

"Yes, it's you." The healer sagged back in the seat.

"Of course it's me. Who did you expect?"

"Never mind," she said. "The important thing is that Queb may be stronger now than he was before," her voice faded.

"Queb'll get you if you don't watch out," Ares muttered softly to himself and then whistled long and low.

"So what's this about his staff?" he asked.

"It was my original mission," she grunted, hunkering lower in the seat.

"Mission?" Ares studied her face intently. "Then you *were* looking for this Queb, weren't you?"

Zelia glanced away quickly.

"You realize you've got an awful lot of explaining to do," Ares said, "assuming we survive."

"Does that mean you'll go back? I can assure you our job here isn't finished yet." Zelia trembled despite the warm sun which penetrated the tangle of vine-laden boughs.

"What's this about a job? I don't remember applying for a job. We never discussed benefits or pension. I just came along for the ride," he quipped. "Besides, I usually make people pay dearly for my services."

"Thanks, I knew I could count on you," she retorted. "The plan is this: we need to go back and destroy his lair, his laboratory and his playthings. We must make sure he has no base from which to operate and that all his creations are dead."

"We? What's this we? You got a frog in your pocket?"

Zelia folded her arms across her chest and glared at him. "All right, you stay behind. I'll do it myself."

"So you're just going to twitch your little finger and the whole citadel will come tumbling down, eh, witch?"

"I saved your miserable hide back there."

"You did? I don't remember that."

"You were out cold," she said.

"And how, pray do tell, did you save this poor miserable adventurer?"

Zelia exhaled in exasperation. "It's too difficult to explain. You still don't understand the mind–body link of magic, or Queb's powers." She tapped her chin, trying to think. "To put it simply, I've destroyed the body, which was already weak and was as much of a prison to him as being immured between the planes, but not the mind. I couldn't have. It was too easy and he's too strong. He could have stopped me any time, but he didn't. Queb would never have permitted his physical destruction unless it worked to his advantage."

"And that saved my hide?"

"After a fashion, yes," she said. "Like I said, you were out cold, and you missed the conversation when he told me that he was going to do just that – abandon his body and take over somebody else's. Disguised, he could walk abroad without causing comment. And stronger, he'd be virtually unstoppable. And whose body do you think he planned to inhabit?"

"Mine," Ares winced. "How did you stop him?"

"I've been trying to work that out. I think when I threw myself over you, I protected you somehow. I know I sensed something . . ." she paused and shuddered ". . . evil hovering above us, and then it . . . just went away. I don't know."

"Well, what about you? How come he didn't take over you? You were convenient," Ares said.

"I don't know," Zelia threw up her hands. "I haven't got all the answers, not yet. I have no idea how the spell was supposed to work. Maybe I escaped by covering my nose and my mouth so I didn't inhale the dust. The answer's probably somewhere in these books, but time's short. Right now he could be slithering into the consciousness of one of his troll-like creations. Brigitta only knows! Now, are you with me or not?"

"I'm going to regret this," Ares groaned. "Okay, let's say I agree. What do you suggest 'we' do? Just go dancing in there alone, me waving my hammer and you brandishing a wand? That sounds like a good way to get spitted and served as a tenday roast."

He got down from the wagon to stretch his legs. "So what do you have in mind? If you tell me I'm supposed to challenge the entire group to duel, count me out!"

"I had something a little more effective in mind."

"Thanks for your vote of confidence," he mumbled.

"How about an explosion?"

"An explosion? How do you propose to whip that one up?"

"I've looked it up." She extracted a spell from the pile on her lap. "I have a powder for fireworks that I picked up in the Abruzzi. I used to use it whenever I wanted to impress my audience. Nothing like a little fireworks to separate a skinflint from his purse."

"A little, you say? It's a whole complex. Do you have enough?"

"I'm not sure," Zelia scowled, "but I've, er, other things to augment it."

"Has it occurred to you that if we're successful we may kill ourselves?"

"We can use some of that slow-burning lichen braided with rags to create a fuse – a long fuse. The lichen should burn, but not too swiftly, and I can ignite it with my wand." She fished it from her pocket. "That will give us more distance. If we leave the wagon here and take your horse, we may just make it."

Ares pondered all aspects of the plan, looking

for a flaw. "Okay, and how do we plant it? I hate to remind you, but there's an entire underground city down there. I mean, we can hardly walk into the cavern and say to the first friendly mutant we meet: 'Excuse us, but we plan to bring this cave down around your ears.' Come on, be reasonable. The inhabitants won't take this lightly. Besides, how do you know you can place it properly so that it will bring down the entire labyrinth?"

"Well, I suggest we go to the wizard's laboratory. I wouldn't be surprised if he had some explosives in his bag of tricks. As for placing it, well, I suppose the closer we get to the base of the structure the more likely we are to be successful."

"This is madness!"

"We'll have to trust in luck."

Ares shook his head. "I hope we haven't used up our share for the day."

His objections voiced, he wandered off to gather lichen, leaving Zelia to rummage through powders and potions. She dragged a can and some Rejuvenator from the shelves, tore open small sachets and poured these into the large tin.

Ares returned, carrying lichen, which he had twisted into a rope. This he wound around his torso and draped over his shoulders and arms.

"How about those vines?" He nodded back over his shoulder. "I bet those would make good fuses."

"Great!" She stuffed as much of the fungal twine as she could into a bag of rags and continued to empty small herbal pouches into the canister, checking the scroll periodically.

Ares tore a vine from a bough and peered from the bottled Rejuvenator to Zelia as she ripped open the seams in the small sachets.

"I don't understand," he indicated the pouches. "You think physick and some love potion might make them more amenable to our little excursion?"

"No, but the physick contains alcohol, which is highly flammable, and if the herbs are mixed properly, they'll enhance the explosives."

"From now on, I think I'll stay away from your potions."

Zelia laughed. "We'll use the Rejuvenator to saturate the rags, and if we don't succeed, well, maybe we can drink ourselves into oblivion."

"You mean before we end with a bang."

"Something like that," she said grimly.

The sun was high overhead as they loaded the warhorse with the sacks and bottles. Ares, wrapped like a Hamadan's mummy in the rope made of lichen, cloth and vines, mounted and offered Zelia a hand up. She refused.

Grabbing the large tin into which she had tipped the many powdered herbs, Zelia climbed gingerly into the wagon's seat and straddled the horse carefully. Ares dug booted heels into the stallion's sides and the beast sprung into a canter. Zelia's mouth closed with a jarring click. They hadn't gone very far when Ares reined in the mount.

"That stuff won't explode, will it? I don't fancy blowing myself up before we've made it to the cavern."

Zelia gave him a round-eyed stare. "Come now, it's been rattling around in the back of the wagon for months. It won't explode."

Ares gave her a terse nod and slapped the stallion's rump with the reins.

"I don't think," she added under her breath.

The cave wasn't difficult to find. They left the stallion and loaded themselves with their supplies. Zelia slung the satchel of clanging Rejuvenator over her shoulder and hugged the tin of explosives to her breast. Ares carried the sack with the lichen and rag ropes. What they hadn't been able to stuff into it, he wore. They clanged into the rocky alcove.

"Stealth!" he snorted. "We'd better hope his creatures are deaf. Can you at least silence the bells, unless you have one specifically to put someone to sleep?"

She flicked her wrist, muffling their clappers, and then elbowed past him. "Step aside, please."

Before Ares had a chance to object Zelia had sent a searing flash to the rocks which hung above the cave's entrance. They came down in a roaring rush. He hollered and jumped sideways, away from the avalanche.

"What did you do that for? You'll wake the dead!"

She turned to him, her expression a mixture of fear and determination. "Just one more exit they can't use."

"And neither can we. You're crazy! How in Hades do you expect to get back to the horse?"

"I have an infallible belief in your sense of direction."

"Remind me to leave you if we survive this."

"As you wish," she replied, unperturbed. "Lead on."

Ares crawled down the small tunnel. Zelia handed him the satchel of Rejuvenator and wriggled along behind. This time, when she demolished the entrance, he wasn't surprised. The wand gave off a feeble glow in the aftermath of power. She murmured a single word and it brightened.

He stood for a second to get his bearings and then strode resolutely in the direction he believed the laboratory to be. She followed, her hand placed to mute the bottles' incessant clatter.

"Here, give it to me." Ares fiddled with them a moment, wrapping the clinking glass with the rags and lichen, and slung them over his shoulder.

Zelia slapped her forehead. "Why didn't I think of that?"

"Can't think of everything," he grunted.

After many bends and turns, Zelia was totally lost, and she was sure Ares was too when he hesitated a moment before motioning at a nail-studded door. "After you."

"You're a genius!" She kissed him.

"If I were such a genius, I wouldn't be here now," he grumbled irritably.

Zelia chortled and summoned fire to light the torches. The gryphon hissed and she silenced it with a sleep spell before starting to browse through the heavily laden shelves. A small cry of joy escaped her lips. She pointed to three large canisters.

"Blasting powder! See, I told you no self-respecting wizard could do without it." She opened one and grinned. "Og provides! We should be able to bring down the entire mountain with this."

"Fine! You realize, of course, that the wagon's only halfway down the mountain."

She didn't respond. Instead she bent over the sorcerer's spellbook, leafing through the pages. Ares went to pull a couple of gowns from a hook.

"We're in luck," Zelia said. "I was right. Our friend Queb created this little citadel. Here's the plans. I can't quite work out how he did it. I don't understand everything; these are difficult to decipher. I can't say much for his penmanship, but it seems there's an oubliette and a storeroom directly below our feet. The entrance," she glanced over her shoulder, "is somewhere in this room."

Ares grimaced and searched the floor for a trapdoor, or a rug which might conceal one.

"I can't see it." He passed her a robe. "Here, disguises. As long as our friends don't see us together they may take us for the wizard."

Zelia shrugged into the scratchy robe, knelt to examine the floor, and knocked over Queb's staff. She scooped it up, stood, and then leaned on it, glowering at the spellbook. Her frown turned into a broad smile. "Ah, ha!"

Zelia tapped the floor three times with the staff and murmured something unintelligible. A pentagram began to glow, outlining the irregularly shaped slabs, and the door was revealed.

Ares moved forward, grabbed the now apparent ring and strained to lift the heavy slate. His muscles bulged and the stone grated slightly, but did not budge.

"Use a lever," Zelia said as she yanked a large kettle from the cold hearth and started to fill it with Rejuvenator. Ares wedged the axe handle under the block, pulled the bottle from her hands and took a healthy swallow.

"Sorry, I needed a bit of a pick-me-up." He wiped his lips with the back of his hand, heaved at the stone and flipped it over and on to the floor with a crash. "Good stuff, that."

Toasting his prowess, Zelia gulped down some of the Rejuvenator before dumping the rags and vines into the kettle. "Look, I'll set the powder. If I read the plans correctly, this room is near the base, or as near as we're going to get. Why don't you scout out the quickest route to the settlement while I work? I can do this alone."

"Okay." Ares tugged at his belt. "It sounds like a good plan to me."

Zelia braided the soaked cloth-rope with the dry lichen. The moist lichen alone wouldn't ignite, but once it was twined with the saturated cloth it should light easily and burn slowly enough that they would have time to escape – or so she hoped.

Once the braid was finished, Zelia climbed down the rickety steps to the storeroom and, from there, down a ladder to the oubliette where she emptied the first canister. She weighted one end of the fuse within the powdery pile with a stone, tied the other end around her waist and climbed to the storeroom to repeat the process. Then she returned to the laboratory, trailing the makeshift fuse behind her.

Ares returned and watched as she wrapped it around a table leg to anchor it.

"The city's not far, but . . ." he scratched his head. "How much of that," he indicated the rest of their supplies, "are we going to have to carry? It would be best if we weren't loaded down."

"The small pot there, two canisters and the fuse, but what's left will fit in both bags."

"How about if I take some of it now, stash it, and come back and get you?"

Zelia gave him a brief nod of assent. "Good. I'm not quite ready," she said.

He placed the remaining canisters in the now-empty satchel and stepped back through the door.

"Wait, take this," she said, pressing a small pot full of noxious green liquid into his hands.

Ares made a wry face and wrinkled his nose in disgust. "What is it?"

"The wizard called it pollution. Remember

the mist? Well, this is what knocked us out. If we add this to the powder, maybe the creatures that survive the blast will suffocate."

"And what about *us*?"

"We'll be gone. We'd better be," she said. "Whatever you do, don't inhale the fumes."

"Now she tells me!" Ares groused as he exited with his burden.

Zelia went to collect the sorcerer's staff. Her original mission was finally completed, and if she was right, now far more important than it had been. As an afterthought, she took Queb's scroll and large spellbook, which she stacked next to the door.

When Ares came back, she slipped through to the hall and handed him the bag of dripping fuses.

"Hold them away from you. That fluid can burn the skin."

Ares took the bag from her, saying, "We *are* in luck. It seems they are day-sleepers. I only saw a few creatures moving about. Let's hope it stays that way. Have you lit the fuse?"

"No, not yet. We'll come back. There are a few things I want to take with me."

"You're crazy!"

"I believe we've established that already." Zelia pushed him gently ahead of her. "Just humour me."

They went down a short hall and clambered over a rubble-strewn mound to reach the main corridor. Large boulders shifted precariously under their weight.

One greasy torch guttered feebly in the gloom, and they paused briefly before the arch where Ares picked up the powder.

"I'll set the powder and fuses. You pour," Zelia said, indicating the mixture in his hands with a jut of her chin. It belched viscously, and Ares made a wry face, freeing a hand to hold his nose. Zelia tied a clean cloth round her face to cover her nose and mouth and, giving him another, motioned that he should do the same. He fumbled with the mask as she moved cautiously to the far wall, where she crammed as much of the powder as she could into a large fissure and then jammed the makeshift fuse into the powder. Ares crept up behind and added a heavy dollop of the nauseating concoction.

Her nimble fingers twined the soaked vine and lichen together for the next batch, and she spoke, her voice muffled by the mask:

"I'm going down below." She pulled her mask away from her mouth to lick the *kymus* from her fingers and rued it. Gagging on the pollution's fumes, she propelled him towards the far side of the shelf and then turned to stumble down the stairs.

Her eyes stung and her hands shook as Zelia performed the last ritual, packing the powder into not one, but several slender crevasses, leaving a thin thread of powder from each to a larger central pile. She fumbled with the fuse, scooping loose powder to cover it. Ares joined her, added his deadly brew and helped her to her feet. They rushed up the stairs.

"Where?" she rasped hoarsely. "Where is it?"

Ares grasped her shoulders and pointed her in the right direction. Blinking the tears away, she spied the serpentine fuse. A light blast and the thing began to sizzle. For a minute she wasn't sure it would catch, but it spluttered, sparked and then flared. She leapt back to light the second.

"Hey!" A voice echoed across the huge cavern. They had been spotted. The time for caution was past.

"Let's get out of here!" she yelled.

Ares seized her arm and ran – not straight ahead, but down a small side corridor. Other shouts mingled with the first bull bellow.

"You'll like this," he said, shoving her through an uneven opening. She lost her footing and fell, sliding on her rump down a steep decline. With a whoop, he followed. They burst through a curtain and landed inside the laboratory.

"The place is full of them, and they all lead

here," he pointed to the floor beneath their feet. "Come on, let's move!"

Ares bolted towards the door with Zelia on his heels. She grabbed the spellbooks, scrolls and amulets and thrust them into Ares' arms. Then she spun to ignite the final fuse. They dashed out of the laboratory, Zelia clutching the sorcerer's staff.

Racing against time, the two plummeted ahead. Sooner than she expected they were crawling along on their stomachs through the blasted exit, to emerge scraped and bleeding at the other side.

"Get rid of the exits! Hah!" Ares sprang into the saddle, almost ripping her arm from the socket as he hauled her up behind him. She twisted to destroy the remaining opening.

Disregarding the trail, Ares steered the beast towards the ledge. Pulling his sword from his sheath, he tapped the stallion's rump with the flat of the blade. Its powerful leg muscles bunched and it hurtled into space, soaring over the low cliff to land with a clop of hooves. Ares gave him rein and the stallion galloped mindlessly ahead, leaving them to dodge low-hanging branches as best they could. The horse careened down the mountain. The sun hung suspended, poised in its flight from the amorous moons. On the opposite horizon, the first moon ascended hazily above the trees. The terrain became a crashing blur of whipping boughs that caught and tore at Zelia's hair. Boulders appeared out of nowhere, and the horse swerved to miss yet another grey trunk. Riding pillion, Zelia clung to Ares for dear life. Her previously silenced chimes screamed shrilly.

Less than five minutes had passed when they plunged headlong into the clearing where they'd left the wagon. Before the destrier had come to a complete halt, Ares sprung from the stallion. Grabbing the reins, he leapt on to Heifer's back and whipped her into motion, and they continued their pell-mell race against time. Their progress was slowed by the trail, which curved and turned this way and that. The wagon bumped noisily over ruts and swayed crazily behind the maddened mare.

The earth sagged beneath them. Then it surged, thrusting upwards. The warhorse reared, his eyes pivoting wildly in his sockets. Zelia fought to keep the steed under control and wheeled him around to face the mountain. The wagon rattled to a stop a few metres later.

"Are you nuts?" he shouted. "Go!"

She shook her head no. "If we're not far enough away by now, we never will be."

The stallion danced sideways, curvetting

nervously. There was a muted boom followed by another. Ares cheered as Zelia slithered from the mount, swearing. She gave him a murderous look. His jubilation withered, and the cry died on his lips.

"No!" she shrieked, enraged. "Demons, Hades' fire and damnation! No!"

The healer stomped around the small glen, the sorcerer's staff still held tightly in her fist. Heifer's sides heaved and her head drooped. Ares reached down to give the horse a reassuring pat as he watched Zelia storm through the brush, punctuating each expletive with a heavy-handed thwack of the stave at the helpless grass nearby. Her bells pealed in sharp counterpoint.

Ares regarded her, amused by the tantrum and amazed by her invective. He was no innocent himself, but this lovely blue maiden was using language which would make a Ticinian sailor blush.

Mildly he interrupted her tirade. "By the great Og, will you tell me what's wrong? The explosives went off and we're still in one piece. What more do you want?"

"It wasn't enough!" she put her hands on her hips and glared at him.

"Not enough?"

"Don't you understand? The place had to be *demolished*. We can't afford to leave anything. No nook, no cranny. Not a single bit of magical paraphernalia. Nothing Queb could use to begin again. Judging by the size of the subterranean city, if we'd been successful, the entire top of the mountain should have collapsed."

Furious, Zelia turned to shake a fist at the mountain, and the healer's bells tolled a strangely dissonant knell. She stared at her wrist, only then becoming aware of the wizard's staff clenched in her hand. Slowly Zelia arched her back, raising the stave high above her head, and then she brought it down to deliver a fracturing blow to the earth beneath her feet.

As the gnarled stick splintered, the mountain imploded!

Boulders the size of small cottages thundered down around them, a lethal grey rain of granite. The rocks bounced and ricocheted, careening through the forest and crushing everything that came in their path. The thick trunks on even the mightiest of ancient oaks snapped like so much fragile glass. Many gave up their turns-long hold on the soil and toppled rigidly, taking other trees with them as they fell. Their exposed roots writhed in an unnatural wind. Those trees that managed to remain standing wobbled crazily. Their limbs waved frantically, while the shrubs shivered and shook as though they had been struck with palsy.

The cumulative roar of crackling trunk and thrashing bough was deafening, and the earth bucked and heaved beneath them. It lifted both the wagon and the horse, throwing the two of them as if they were little more than children's toys. A fissure opened between Zelia's legs. She dived sideways, belly down, and rolled away from the fracture. She clambered to her hands and knees, ready to scramble to one side or the other should another chasm open beneath her.

The deadly shower continued, raining everywhere except on them, as if they were somehow immune. Zelia's head swivelled round and she gaped at Ares. A brilliant white glow emanated from him, enveloping them both. He looked as though he were on fire. The boulders crashed harmlessly around them. The adventurer had encased them in a protective shield. His eyes were focused elsewhere, on some nether-world beyond her ken. Feet firmly planted on the churning earth, the mercenary rode its surging as one would ride a bucking horse. The blinding aura expanded, stretching outwards. The rocks caromed off this unearthly shell with a dreadful clacking, and Zelia placed her hands over her ears, cringing away from the luminous Ares and the deafening noise.

The onslaught slackened, the chunks of granite shrinking from the size of a house to that of a horse, then a man. Boulders became rocks, rocks became stones, and then pebbles – until all that fell was a fine powder.

Zelia stood on trembling legs. Amazed, she watched as the shimmering shield flashed briefly and then went out. They were trapped within a pen of boulders and debris that formed a perfect circle of stone around them and the wagon.

The dust that Ares' power had held at bay rushed in, filling the vacuum his spell had created. The air clogged. Zelia sputtered while Ares shook himself as though waking from a dream. He turned to her, dazed. A branch dislodged itself from the ring of earth and stone that surrounded them and toppled down on top of her. Zelia felt a sharp pain, and all went black.

A gentle voice spoke her name and warm arms encircled her. She could feel the thump of a heart beating close to hers, and she extended her arms to embrace the possessor of the voice.

"You saved my life," she said. Ares covered her lips with his own. They parted briefly. Zelia silenced her bells with a wave of her hand. He kissed her again before lowering her tenderly to the ground.

* * *

Zelia plucked twigs from her hair and stared at him. "You could have run, you know. You didn't have to come after me. Why did you?"

Ares raised himself up on his elbow to peer into her face. "Let's just say that insanity runs in the family."

"Let's not," she scowled as he played with a strand of her hair. "It's been clear to me that you have accompanied me for some other reason besides companionship. Sometimes when you don't think I'm looking, I can see an expression on your face that makes my blood run cold. Like a predator eyeing its prey. At times, I've been convinced that you hated me."

"Hate you? No, not hate you." Ares twisted the blue curl around his finger. "Envy you, yes, but not hate."

"Why would you envy me? I am hunted. I am despised for the same reasons you are, and then some. I can see nothing for you to be jealous of."

"Your magic," he said simply.

"My magic? What about it?"

"I wish I had it. I can feel its working. I can see it. I've always been able to. I can even see the silvery, tenuous light of the grid, but I cannot touch it. I cannot manipulate magic as you can," Ares said. "Your magic drew me. I don't know why or how. It drew me all the way from Norvon to Pelopnos. At least, I think it did."

"Yes, I sensed your pursuit," she said.

"If you did, then I'm losing my touch."

"No, magically, I mean."

"Could you teach me?"

"Sorcery?" Zelia waggled her fingers at Ares. "Why?" she whispered. "Why would you want to be like me? I'm an outlaw."

"Outlaw, ha! Rules are made to be broken," he said.

"I've always thought that. Now I'm not so sure. I wonder if you'll feel the same once you've been tied to the stake, or when the flames lap up your feet to your thighs."

He avoided her eyes. "You risk it."

"I can't help what I am."

"Well, neither can I." The adventurer sat up. Speaking softly, Ares told her of his dream, of the woman with hair every bit as white as his own.

Zelia shook her head. "So you think that means you can't return to your people until you have magic of your own?"

"What else can it mean?"

She wanted to tell him it could be no more than a vision a lonely child might conjure up in search of a long-lost mother. Hadn't she cherished such a dream? One look at his earnest expression, and she bit her tongue.

"Every time I've tried to find my people, I got lost in the mists," Ares mused out loud.

"But you do have magic of your own. How else could you have done what you did?"

"What did I do?" he asked.

She gestured at the stone wall whch encircled them. Folding his arms across his chest, Ares surveyed the enclosure and lifted his shoulders with a shrug. "I did that?"

"You don't remember?"

"No," he said.

The blue maiden gazed at him sadly. "I'm afraid I cannot teach you. I wouldn't know how. I am untrained myself, but I will do what I can. I will instruct you in the language of mages. You can watch. You can read my scrolls. Maybe you can teach yourself, much as I have taught myself."

He beamed at her, reached out to take her hand and shook it heartily. "Agreed. Now, how do you suggest we get out of here? How about a little sorcery?"

"Magic doesn't work like that."

"I was afraid you'd say that."

Had it not been for the horses and the wagon, they could easily have scaled the barricade, but neither animal could have made it over the loose scree. Zelia tried a few futile blasts, but they did little more than pulverize rock into pebble and pebble into powder, turning the wall to sand. They used the remaining daylight hours to clear one side of their stone prison, laboriously piling heavy stone upon heavy stone. A large mound had been erected in the centre of the broken circle, and the one side reduced to a pile of rubble. They hitched the wagon to both horses and eventually managed to haul it out. By the time they were finished, a purple blanket covered the sky, and they were too exhausted to continue.

"Do you think some day someone will find this and think it's a portal?" Ares said as they slumped next to each other against the rocky wall.

"I don't know, but that," she thumbed at the empty horizon where a mountain had once stood, "will probably keep the mapmakers busy for a while."

Their eyes were glazed with exhaustion, their faces smudged with dirt. Flames sent the leaping shadows in a jigging dance among the heaped stones. Zelia settled into a light trance, casting about them for a trace of Queb's power, some residual that said he continued to exist, but Ares' strong hand fell heavily on her shoulder and wrenched her spirit back into her body. Zelia flinched away from him.

"None of that," Ares said. "You've still got

some explaining to do. It's pretty obvious to me that you weren't at all surprised by what we found back there. You knew what you were doing. You *knew* who and what we were dealing with all along, didn't you?"

"I wouldn't exactly say I knew what I was doing," she rubbed scalded eyes with her thumb and forefinger, "but, yes, I knew who he was. I've been looking for him all these months."

Head tilted to one side, Ares gave her a searching look and nodded. "It makes sense. As eccentric as it seemed, I always thought your path was somehow planned, as if you had some secret purpose. I certainly didn't think you'd stopped at the Northern Wastes just so that I could relive my lost youth. You're not what you seem to be, are you, Zelia renegade cleric? How much of what you told me is true?"

"Most of it, I suppose."

"Are you a healer or aren't you?"

"I am, but then again I'm not, or I don't think I am," she faltered. "I don't know."

"Don't know? How can you not know? You either are or you aren't. You said you were expelled."

"Yes, I killed the slaver and then I healed him." Ares nodded as if he understood. "I suppose you might say I reformed him, or the close scrape with death certainly did. Now he's a used-dung-camel salesman." Ares rolled his eyes heavenward.

"Hey," she went on. "It was the best I could do, quality of the cloth, you know. Anyway, he's got no memory of a former life." She hesitated. "As for expelled, well, I don't know if it's official."

Ares threw up his hands in frustration. With a sigh, Zelia lifted a leather thong from beneath her tunic and showed him the heavy brass bell she wore. Ares reached out to examine it. When he flipped it over to scrutinize the carving on the opposite side, the clapper fell – without making a sound.

"You see, I'm the successor to the High Priestess of Brigitta. The bell is silenced until I can again reclaim my office." Zelia winced. "The Matriarch has sent me out to find Queb and steal his staff. Quite unofficially, of course. It's a wizardly affair, but since they choose to ignore it, the healers must act. Covertly."

Ares let the bell drop soundlessly on its leather thong.

"You could say I'm a spy. I was sent to obtain proof that Queb exists and roams the world once more. That he is not some figment of a female's feverish imaginings . . . and . . . we couldn't let anyone know what I was going to do. The wizards don't take interference kindly," she explained. "So you see, I had to get free of the cloister. I *had* to be expelled."

"But you said you weren't sure if the expulsion was official."

"And I'm not. The Matriarch went through a sham rite of anathema before 'impartial' witnesses. I don't know how she did it, but she even managed to find a Shamirian crystal that was similar to mine and shattered it as the ritual requires. She thought that if I were to disappear she might be able to prevent the formal hearing, but I don't know if she was successful on that one. So you see, I don't know if I've been officially expelled or not."

"If you *have* been expelled, how can you remain as heir?"

"Bylaws, I suppose. The choice is hers and hers alone. No one can gainsay her."

"Why you? Why not someone less valuable?"

"My powers, I suppose. My less than orthodox talents."

"You mean set a thief to catch a thief?"

Zelia pursed her lips. "It's not how I would have chosen to phrase it, but yes, something like that. It sounded exciting at the time. I'm not what you might call the contemplative type, and I get tired of the cumbersome robes and the even more onerous formalities of rank and privilege. I didn't really fit in. I never have. The Matriarch seems to think it's my special quest. Somehow she's got it into her mind that it's my destiny to face this wizard. She sees it as some kind of divine mission and is convinced that whatever has to be accomplished can only be accomplished by me," she paused, "but I think she's flipped her wimple on this one."

Zelia waved the wizard's broken staff in the air. "Well, I've got our proof, but I'm out of my element here."

"So you've been looking for this necromancer every night when you . . ." Ares tapped her temple and then made fluttering motions with his fingers, thrusting his arms skyward to simulate flight.

"How did you know what I was doing?"

He shrugged. "I told you I can see these things. I can recognize a spell upon the winds the same way I can predict an enemy's action. Maybe it has something to do with these," and he tugged at a delicately pointed ear.

"And today?"

Indicating the stone enclosure, Ares said, "I don't remember a thing. I remember a bang, seeing the boulders, thinking that this was it, and steeling myself to die. If I did what you said I did, then I can't tell you how. I have no talents that I know of beyond a certain awareness."

Zelia gazed at him for a moment and accepted his statement with a quick duck of her head. "You say you can predict your opponents' next move. Maybe your power only manifests itself in moments of extreme danger."

"You insult my swordsmanship." His eyes narrowed and he glared into the fire.

"Surely you've met someone during your career who was a little stronger, a little faster, a little better than yourself?"

"Of course, and I fought like a demon to keep my skin intact." He prodded his flat abdomen. "I never did think it would look good full of holes or with someone else's sword sticking out."

"And then did you use this ability to stay alive?" she asked.

"Certainly. Who wouldn't?"

"I rest my case."

"No, I don't agree. I've been in danger before – it's part and parcel of my trade." His hand went to his battle hammer and the grizzly belt. "But I've never done anything particularly spectacular."

"Well, take my word for it. What you did today *was* spectacular."

"Perhaps it's something more than that. I've always been alone in the past, with no one to protect but myself." The line between his brows deepened and he gave her a sidelong glance.

Zelia's breath caught in her throat and her heart fluttered like a caged bird in her breast. She retreated from his searching gaze and peered into the cheery blaze. The firewand burrowed deeper into her pocket, snugged against her flank and thrummed contentedly.

"One thing's for sure – I'm not strong enough to face him alone," she said. "I've got to have help."

"You think he's still alive, then?"

"I do." Zelia's shoulders drooped dejectedly and she fastened tormented eyes on Ares' face. "And I must return to Pelopnos, where I have a price on my head. You're not involved yet, so this is a good time to leave. Get out while you can – I wouldn't blame you if you did. I don't particularly relish the idea of getting roasted on a spit."

The fire danced and crackled, filling the palpable silence.

Ares plucked playfully at her hand. "What? And miss all the excitement? They'd drum me from the adventurers' guild if I did that!"

CHAPTER 12

Something dark and sinister vacated the empty shell to swoop down on unsuspecting maid and man. The healer threw herself over the still form of her partner, and it withdrew. It circled around her like a faint zephyr, to find her hand tightly clamped over her nose and mouth.

Entrance denied! Without a mouth to scream with, all Queb could do was retreat, wailing silently.

It must find a home; the wizard was too new to this game to control this formless void. A wisp of himself detached itself from the rest. Queb imagined a large arm reaching out and clutching the tendril of consciousness back to his breast, and it scurried home, nestling close to his non-existent side.

The disembodied spirit darted down the long hall, prodding this consciousness and that, until it found one with the few rudiments of intelligence. He made a bee-line for a mouth. The beast opened its eyes and started to scream, for Queb had picked one of the injured guards. He quit this tainted home and his search began anew.

Here and there, he dithered across the vast cavern, seeking a temporary domicile, testing this creature, then that, and abandoning each as they proved inadequate for his needs. Bits of himself tried to sneak off, and he raged, for the necromancer sensed the flight of the fay duo the way the wolf senses the flight of the deer.

All right, he thought, *if not intelligence, then size! Brawn!* He'd throttle them if he could not have them otherwise. The wizard settled on a snoozing guard. His entry was none-too-gentle. The creature shot upright, did a sidewise jig, spun a couple of times, and crumpled.

Kaboom!

Queb felt his new body being blown into tatters. Rocks were flying everywhere, and the wizard was in very real danger of losing parts of himself and getting tangled in the debris.

He collected himself and zeroed in on the next available creature as it lumbered along.

Kaboom! KABOOM! Flames shot out, igniting the frenzied beast.

"Oh, no!" he howled. This time he was able to form lips in the middle of the leaping pyre that enveloped his temporary abode.

Queb evacuated the burning shell. Another loped past, and the wizard latched on. The animal dropped, useless to him now, overcome by pollution's fumes.

The disembodied consciousness hovered above them. Little more than an ink stain in the velvet-black night, it remained unobserved by the couple below even when its shadow blotted out the fat crescent of the fourth moon. The girl still could not sense him unless he wanted her to, and the sorcerer realized that the daughter was only a shadow of his ancient guardian and adversary, Astra Aurelius.

It flitted this way and that, outside the bounds of protective wards, trying to find a chink in this psychic armour. It drifted, listening to the couple as the renegade healer surmised, correctly, his purpose.

The wench was smarter than he thought. The necromancer attempted to throw a spell which would blast the couple from this dimension, but without fingers to point or arms to gesticulate, the spell bounced impotently off the warded circle.

Unused to this new manifestation the spirit was blown like tatters, shredding before a gentle breeze. The transformation was as yet incomplete. The whirling cloud that was Queb descended as close to the protective shield as he dared to flutter over the wagon. The mare pranced skittishly, sensing what her mistress did not. The spirit that once was Queb pressed against the magical aegis, spreading himself as thin as he had ever been between planes, and set about to memorize every curve and line of the loathsome features.

The airy elemental made flesh.

Before escaping into the night, he swore her death would be as painful a one as he could imagine. Out of sorts, the wizard didn't appreciate the irony that this spirit-form rode upon the elemental's airy wings, spreading death in its wake.

The sheik gazed at the barren plain and grimaced. People from the north always complained about the windswept deserts of Daklha, but the southern continents had nothing like this. Laden with quartz fragments, the sandy dunes glittered under the wide open eye of the southern sun, but here there was naught but grey clouds which swam low in the firmament.

They had been here and gone. Their straggling path looped from the main road far to the southeast to this gods-forsaken place. From this position he could view the dusty trail of their return, heading due west, and he wondered what had possessed his daughter to roam into this lifeless land. Thunder rumbled somewhere, and the sheik knelt as if, by examining their path, he could discern their intent. Obviously, they had not chosen to tarry here. The ruts made by the wagon were not deep, and if the storm clouds that had threatened to spit rain all day had already released their content, the sheik probably would have lost all trace of them.

Zelia's fine stallion snorted and stamped its disapproval of this savage place. The sheik rose and stroked the animal's muscular neck to calm him. He walked around the circle once, then twice, shaking his head.

After completing the last circuit, he halted to stand next to the skittish beast. He twined the reins around his hand and placed a foot in the stirrup ready to mount, when something popped behind him. More than a pop, really – more like a small explosion. The pressure was such that his lungs were compressed – the air pushed out of him in a whistling rush – and then released – and it went whistling back in again – and his ears pinged as if they were being squeezed.

The warhorse pawed at the heavens, and the sheik was thrown and dragged a short way, his hand still wrapped in the reins. There was a ripping noise, and the man's eyes widened in surprise as the sturdy bridle tore in half, loosing the frightened mount. The beast turned tail and ran, steering for the distant mountains.

The bewildered sheik watched the fleeing shadow with a sinking heart and rubbed his sore hand. Laughter reverberated around the circle of stones. The sheik spun and dropped into a defensive crouch, his scimitar raised protectively before him.

A cyclone roared deep within the circle's stony heart. A whirling ball of air, dust, and – intermittently – body parts. As the sheik watched, a mouth, a leg, an arm and an eye would appear, form, reform and then shatter.

A voice boomed, as much inside his mind as out of it. The sheik covered his ears with his hands. It echoed loudly inside his skull.

"So you come to rescue the fair maid and, perhaps, to slay me. Puny mortal! We have met already, your daughter and I. It is your daughter who helped me, giving me the strength to capture you now."

There was a short burst of hilarity from the boiling cloud. "Such a sweet morsel! A tasty treat."

A mouth appeared at the side of the circling wind. It opened slowly as the voice continued to speak. "I will use you to lure her to me, and then I shall devour her, and her powers will be mine for ever."

The spinning cloud rushed towards him, zooming between the two stones with cold blast of air. The cloth of his long-flowing burnous flapped wildly around his ankles. Meanwhile the gaping maw widened until it looked as if the whirlwind was going to split in two. Before the sheik could move or run, he was surrounded by dozens of sharp teeth and purple lips, and found himself looking down the gullet to oblivion. Within a twinkling of an eye, the cyclone enveloped him totally. As he struggled his body made an imprint against the membranous exterior that seemed to hold the wind together. Cold, wet and pliable, like a sodden blanket, it covered his nose and mouth, suffocating him.

And now the sheik was inside the twittering mirth, ingested by nightmare and each sniggering chuckle sucked the air from his lungs. He screamed, and screamed, and screamed. He screamed endlessly, but no sound emerged from his throat.

Everything went grey around him. Then grey faded to black. A resonance vibrated from within the hurricane – a deep belch and a sigh.

There was another soft poof, but no one remained to hear it. The circle of stone was empty, the horse just a dark dot on the horizon. Thunder rumbled and rolled overhead, and it began to rain.

Once beyond the mountains, Ares and Zelia turned immediately south, all their energy bent on returning to the Learned Isle with due course and speed, but their pace was slow. Even the elements seemed to conspire against a hasty advance. A cool spring had turned to a soggy summer. The wagon often got bogged down on the muddy roads, and many times they were forced to stop and extricate the hapless Heifer from the mire. The weather dampened even Flighty's normally querulous spirits, and the hen perched, ruffled against the cold and amazingly silent, under the relentless drizzle.

Another day found their progress arrested on the banks of the Bear's Fork where the road took them towards Ticino. Thunder clapped overhead. Frowning, Zelia looked up. A large raindrop fell with a splat on her face. A boy sprawled beneath her along this deserted stretch of road. His skin was the characteristic grey, and thick catarrh ran from his nose and mouth. He groaned and clutched at her hand. She recognized his costume as one of Ticino and not Uri.

The merciful would have speeded such a child along his way with a dagger or a sword. The greedy would have stripped him and sold his threadbare garments at the market. The couple had seen more than a few naked, bloated bodies along the road – those who were beyond the help of any but the gods who made them.

Because of their need for haste, Zelia tried to turn a blind eye to their suffering, but the bells of office carried with them the weight of responsibility. So their journey was delayed over and over again as she halted to chase the demon of disease through wasted flesh.

For the past week they had seen scores of people leaving the city-state of Ticino – men, women and children, always travelling alone – and Zelia knew they fled plague itself, thinking it safe beyond Uri's borders. But the malady they hoped to escape had started in the north and been brought south during spring raids of the Szatmar tribes along the Uri coast.

The refugees from the north crashed like a surging sea against those fleeing the south, and the contagion spread. They all had similar symptoms. No herb, no trick of crystal or chime cured them. The best the lone healer could do was ease their pain, for it was beyond her meagre skills, and as Zelia looked south, she wondered how they fared at the college.

She rocked back and forth weakly, drawing on already overtaxed powers, and placed both hands on the child's forehead. Again she sent a questing search throughout the pain-racked body, noting, as she had in the past, the body's slow rebellion against itself. Zelia ranged deeper, feeling, sensing *something,* something dark, some key just beyond her grasp, yet still it eluded her.

The water seeped into the knees of her leather leggings. Zelia leaned back to rest on her heels, letting the rain soak through her cloak. Her eyes were lined with red, and she felt as if someone had dropped a hot coal beneath each lid. All the healer wanted to do was crawl back into the wagon and dry off, but she tried again, sighing wearily and letting her hands rest lightly on the child's head.

Ares gazed down at her anxiously, smiling encouragement. He squatted next to her and placed a reassuring hand on each shoulder. She stiffened, eyes wide as his energy ran through her like a roaring river current, washing away all fatigue. Ares' touch, Ares' mind, came with her, augmenting her powers and directing them. His vitality swept like a wave, swelling and pouring through her to the child. Again Zelia followed the same long path throughout his fevered body, pursuing the course of the disease to its source.

For an instant, she found herself face to face with a shade of Hades itself. It appeared to her as a warped ghoulish figure that slavered over the diminishing light which was the child's frail soul. The monstrous vision opened a gaping maw to devour the tenuous flicker, and Zelia vowed that this creature would not have him. The plague's minion straightened, as if noticing her wavering presence for the first time. White light streamed through her. It screamed at her and fled, with a curse.

Something snapped within her mind, and Zelia was again hunched over the little boy, rain running into her eyes. The child squirmed beneath her. She sat up, shaking herself from her torpor. The boy struggled to his feet, his colour the warm pink of the northern Ticino and his fever evidently abated. Zelia grabbed the child and crushed him to her chest.

Beside her, Ares stared, slack-jawed, first at Zelia, then at the child, and then at his trembling hand. "What h-happened?" he asked.

"We did it! We! You and I. I don't know how." She pushed the boy away from her to examine him sceptically, looking for signs of contagion, but she saw none. "I don't care. It worked," she said as she freed the wriggling lad. She hid her face from Ares as she blinked away scalding tears of relief.

Care had worn new lines in the Matriarch's already gaunt features. Behind her, the dying moaned. Every bed in the temple's hospice was full. Some held two, even three, patients. Groaning corpses – those who didn't yet have the sense to lie down and die – wandered through the halls. Those too weak to move and too late for a bed littered every hallway and every classroom in the college.

All healers, no matter how vaunted their position, had been called upon to treat the ailing, and still it was not enough. Nothing worked – no note, no crystal, no song. Not even the curative waters of the crystal pond helped. Herbal remedies sometimes silenced a hacking cough or lowered a fever, but all for naught because the patient died anyway.

Novice, initiate and acolyte alike wore haunted, ghostly expressions, their eyes shaded with dark circles of fatigue as they worked among the dying, and *they* were the healthy ones. The sickly took their place among the patients soon to die. The Matriarch's shoulders trembled as she coughed – a dry, hacking affair that shook her entire body. She knew she was now numbered among the sick and dying, but she could not rest. As Matriarch she could afford neither the luxury nor the time.

Her body stiffened and she held herself rigidly erect, moving cautiously as though she were made of fragile glass. The priestess passed a weary hand over her forehead and whispered a light heal spell to still the racking cough. She skirted the corpses outside the temple door that awaited the next death cart. They would have a long wait. He who had driven it on its gruesome rounds was dead. Fidhl joined her, eyes demurely downcast, and they headed across the forecourt for the Wizards' College.

The Grand Inquisitor swayed in the guttering torchlight. The dim light did little to relieve the gloom in this central chamber. The shutters were closed against the insipid illumination of another watery day. Rags had been stuffed into every crevice or crack which might have admitted either air or light. The room was thick with incense.

The Matriarch peered myopically into the umbra and sniggered humourlessly behind her hand. Such precautions were useless, for it seemed the contagion that rampaged about Eubonia was borne upon the very air they breathed. No amount of smoke could mask it. No amount of rags could prevent its entrance. People carried it with them on their persons. No shutters could block it out. The disease would find them, no matter how hard they tried to evade it.

The Inquisitor raised his arms. His blue-black sleeves decorated with gilt fell back to reveal sinewy arms, whose pale flesh made white smudges in the dusky chapel. The man's fine baritone carried easily to the furthest corners of the crowded chamber.

"Let no law-biding man receive them, or feed them, or give them shelter from the night. Let no one, noble or peasant, give them succour. We name them damned. Damned by all the gods. Damned and heretic," he intoned. "Let them find no rest under the seven planets and the five moons. Curse the food they drink, the ground upon which they walk, and any home where they lay their heads."

The Matriarch wheezed and Fidhl, her assistant, plucked at her sleeve. "Mistress, you should not be here."

She shook him off, her gaze riveted on the Inquisitor as he pronounced the sentence.

People's memories are short and the maid had been all but forgotten as soon as other issues – petty bickering and promotions – had taken precedence.

Then a stupendous force had unhinged magic's balance.

'Twas said that wild sorcery had brought on the plague which ravaged the land with the rapacity of fire elementals on dry grass. 'Twas believed that it was sorcery of such magnitude and power that it had ripped a hole between worlds. And in truth, fairies had been seen in Szatmar and Firth and reported as far south as Shalop and Ticino.

Rumours filtered through slowly from distant lands, proclaiming the gifts of the magical blue maiden and her silver-haired compatriot who could heal a disease none others could, and suddenly the wizards remembered the renegade cleric and her unusual skills.

And *this* was their response to the first faint whisper of cure, of hope. Their response to powers that exceeded their own. To name Zelia and her companion heretic and have them burned in absentia. Her gaze rested upon the twin effigies that hung from the ceiling.

"For their heresies, they are branded heretic. May the fire of sorcery's righteous wrath consume the candle flame of their spirits even as their bodies are consumed upon the pyre." The Archmage and the Inquisitor thrust their torches at the images, and the straw ignited with a whoosh. "And once consumed, may the light of their spirit be extinguished."

With a swoosh of heavy robes, the Inquisitor's arms dropped and every torch in the room was doused.

Some answer! But the sorcerers would have their scapegoat and would not listen to her pleas. The woman turned stony eyes upon the eunuch, and he swung his hands in an expressive gesture of futility. *Fidhl had been right. It was hopeless.*

The Crown of Brigitta exhaled with a long susurrating sigh that turned into a rasping cough. She ambled from the grand chapel, her head bowed under the weight of the truth that the wizard refused to hear. Acolyte and priestess walked in leaden silence across the marble forecourt. Breathlessly, the Matriarch paused outside the Great Circle that marked a sort of no-man's-land between the administrative offices of Healers' and Wizards' Colleges, and murmured a small prayer to Brigitta, asking for strength to face one more day before her body too succumbed to this devilish disease.

* * *

The rains worsened. The river's dark waters swelled and burst angrily from the banks, wiping out the little travelled road, and people moved to higher ground. The damp weather added to their misery. The sodden party wound their way through the fertile Ticino farmland, helping those they could, but the maid and her partner were just two against a rising torrent.

Their journey was made no easier by the posters that adorned every tree, every gallows pole and every village along the high road. The wizards had offered a sizeable reward for the couple's capture – large enough that Ares had teasingly suggested they turn each other in as the most profitable, and speediest, way of getting to Pelopnos. Zelia and Ares bantered lightly, as was their way, each outlining how the bounty would be spent, but they no longer lingered to add drooping moustaches or a jaunty goatee to their portraits.

By tacit agreement, Ares and Zelia took to the forests, for neither of them were easy to lose in a crowd. Only when they were cloaked and hooded under voluminous grey capes could they pass unhindered. Even then they looked odd, such clothing being unseasonable for this time of year, and they had to take care lest a sudden gust of wind expose their features.

Ares urged Zelia to use her magic to speed them along their way, or at least to disguise their persons; but sorcery, like healing, had rules. A spell could transform inanimate matter, but not intelligent life, for to do so would change its essence. Such changes were permanent and neither Zelia or Ares wanted to be something other than what they were. The best that could be done to change living matter was to mask the exterior and that required a continuous expenditure of power that would soon exhaust the user.

Their circuitous route had taken them far from the cities and they found themselves following the same path as before. Sadly, Zelia left the wagon at the first farmhouse they came across, the farmer only too happy to oblige. And now they rode alone by night. The peasants she had once helped gave them shelter, harbouring them from wizardry's long arm. So protected had they been that they had grown lax, and thus it was that they found themselves trapped inside the walled town of Rabnick at night when the tumult started.

A thick fog wrapped itself around their ankles, twining like a cat, as Ares and Zelia huddled in a doorway, arguing. Cressets flickered overhead, and the rumble of the rioters was still distant.

"Do you really think we can get a room

without being recognized? You with your snow-white hair and I with my . . ."

The noise drew closer. An urchin raced shouting up the cobbled street, and Zelia looked up. Her sentence died stillborn. Where one came, others would surely follow.

She glanced back at him. "I don't like this place. I just want to get out of here."

"Well, if you can't magick us away, what do you suggest? What do you want to do? Leap over the walls? Or perhaps you'd like to try your luck with the guards? I think we'd be better off with the local landlord."

The clamour of angry human voices was amplified. They were only a street or so away. Soon the mob would spill all around them. There was a crash somewhere, and the rumble turned into a roar as the crowd surged on to the street.

Zelia held up a warning finger and stepped from the shadows to get a better look. It was a mistake. A group of irate citizens rounded the corner at the same moment as she left the safety of the darkened doorway. She was exposed. They hesitated before this grey phantom, eyeing her distrustfully. A hush fell. In that unguarded instant, her bells chimed softly, betraying her.

"Healer!" someone shouted, pointing, and she jumped away from the crowd. Her hood fell away from her face, exposing the dark blue hair and delicate features.

"Heretic!" shrieked another, recognizing her. Ares darted from his hiding place, his great hammer clenched in his upraised fist, war cry issuing from his lips. The people balked, flinching away from the white-haired apparition. The black cloak billowed about him, revealing the belt of scalps, and some people dithered, looking down at their toes.

"Run!" he barked at her, and she bolted. As if the movement had broken their thrall, the crowd growled again in rage and rushed at Ares. He considered the swelling wall of human flesh for a moment, shrugged, looped his hammer back on to his back and fled. The adventurer raced fleetly along beside Zelia, urging her on.

Behind them, the citizens moved as one beast, with a single mind and intent. Their booted footsteps sounded like thunder against the cobbled streets. Zelia dodged sideways to avoid a discarded corpse and tripped, falling into Ares. He reached out a hand to steady her. Their fingers linked and a current ran between them, the same jolting energy that they knew in a healing trance; but now there was no child to cure, no ailing grandmother to treat. It had no outlet. Zelia wondered if they would be burned up in the aftermath of power, but she had no time to meditate on this.

The world spun and dipped crazily about them. Zelia heard the booming steps, the angry growl, of the enraged populace. She saw the bobbing light of their torches, and then nothing. A blackness, a blankness, a void took them in, shielding them from all. And it was cold, so cold.

The next thing she knew they were rolling tip over tail in wet grass outside the walls of the city. Zelia performed another graceless somersault as Ares flopped next to her, dropping with a grunt. The healer raised herself gingerly from the ground and looked around. They had landed near their camp. Their horses whickered softly in the trees.

"I'm afraid to ask," Ares said in a deceptively matter-of-fact tone. "What sort of trick was that we just did?"

Pushing the hair out of her face with a sharp chatter of bells, Zelia stared at him a while before speaking. "I don't know. If we did what I think we did, taking a shortcut between planes, it's impossible."

"That's nice." Ares stood to offer her a hand up, then stared at his open palm, blanched and turned away without comment.

Thick mists cloaked the docks of Abruzzi in a wet, grey blanket. Ares and Zelia stood alone, listening to the steady drip-drip-drip of condensation. Heifer snorted and sidled coquettishly closer to Ares' great destrier. Below their feet, the sea sloshed sleepily through the great pilings. All was quiet. Too quiet. No sailor's *kvass*-thickened voice disturbed the predawn light. No dogs barked, no children cried. Shivering, Zelia peered into the thick soup that obscured the Isle of Learning.

"Well, now what?" Ares asked.

They stepped apart and looked at each other, so much left unspoken in that pregnant question.

There was no jest about them now. They were about to enter the lion's den, to return to the place where they had been condemned – where they were most sought and most reviled. If they were to survive the attempt, they must leave the docks before it got light; before the pier became crowded with porters, carters and workmen; even before the first ferry took the first band of traders from Abruzzi to Thessalia. In the countryside and in the villages they had been protected, but in the cities tempers ran high, and here in Abruzzi the colleges' influence was strong.

Their eyes locked. Ares' odd pupils had widened to ovals. He winked at her and turned to their mounts to retrieve their lumpy packs, stuffed full of amulets, talismans and scrolls of true power. Zelia extracted Queb's staff from the saddle. She had repaired it with a meld spell, but the crack was still visible. She hoped that, tuned to Queb's vibrations, the stick would lead her to its master, but she had been unable to bend it to her will. It came with her voluntarily, and that frightened her more than any apparent reluctance. The latter could be expected. The maid wondered if the staff had ever in fact bowed to Queb's will. Somehow she doubted it.

The stick buzzed a warning. It had no great love for the wizards' city. Zelia brought it against the ground with a sharp smack to silence its complaint. She didn't like returning to the island any better than it did, but she had no choice. It crackled in wordless rebuke, and she glowered at it as she hooked her pack over her shoulder.

"You ready?" Ares asked.

"I think so," she replied. Her eyes strayed over the mist-shrouded water.

"Do you think we can do it?"

"We've done it before," Zelia said, not lifting her gaze from the swirling grey vapours.

"But never this far."

"What other choice do we have? And if we fail . . ." Her voice was a low murmur, and his eyes followed hers to peer at the roiling wall of fog.

"'Tis a better death than burning, don't you think?" he said.

"Aye," she agreed.

Cradling the staff in her arm, Zelia tore her gaze away from the sea. They linked hands. Again two pairs of eyes sought each other, forging a bond between body, mind and soul. The healer fixed the image of the entrance to the Wizards' College firmly in her mind. Ares plucked the picture from her brain and recited to himself the verbal description she had given when they first planned this mad venture. The horses shifted and neighed softly as their masters began to waver and thin, then vanish.

Somehow they got it wrong, for they reappeared handspans above the marble courtyard only to plummet and fall with a sickening plop into a pile of rotting corpses.

Zelia gagged and struggled into a sitting position. Ares rolled from their cloying roost, dropping to the ground. As she looked about her, Zelia realized with a horrifying shock that the reverse could have happened. They could just as easily have appeared several handspans below the earth, embedded up to their knees in marble and up to their noses in bodies. Then she vomited.

"Gawd!" Ares brushed frantically at his jerkin, trying to wipe away the stench. A chink of iron mail resounded softly in the mist and he belly-flopped, diving into the pile to lie as still as death itself. Zelia flattened herself against a desiccated apprentice, her stomach threatening to unload itself of its contents a second time.

Two guards meandered past, studiously ignoring the heap of human rubbish.

Chink, chink, chink.

Eyes closed, Zelia listened as the sound of armour became muted by the enveloping mist. Carefully, she crawled from her place atop the mound. Over each staring face, she whispered a silent prayer of goddess blessing to speed their troubled spirits on their way. Ares fished himself out from among the bodies and glanced at her, grimacing.

"Maybe this wasn't such a good idea, after all. How are you feeling?"

In answer to his question, she dropped in an ungraceful heap to the marble piazza. Her head spun. They leaned weakly against each other and began a staggering walk towards the locked entrance. Just outside the door, they halted. He turned to her. "Again?"

"You mean to get through the door? Do you think you could do it?"

Ares shook his head no, and again considered the thick, nail-studded door.

"How do we get in?" he asked.

"Why don't we try something original? Let's knock."

With a mirthless chuckle, he nodded. "What a novel idea!"

She raised the staff and rapped soundly against the heavy wood. The boom rebounded hollowly around the marble forecourt, and they waited. Her courage evaporated a little bit more with each passing moment.

This was madness! The wizards had retreated to their citadel while the plague raged about the land. They sought solace in scapegoats and here she was turning herself – themselves, she corrected herself – in to their persecutors. An open invitation to toss them on the pyre, trussed up and ready for roasting.

Sandalled feet scraped the marble paving beyond the door. Zelia steeled herself for confrontation, and behind her she heard the soft hiss of a blade being withdrawn from its sheath. The door creaked slowly open. A monk squinted at them, his eyes fogged with sleep. Then the light of recognition dawned in his vapid, vacuous face. His eyes cleared, just as the first rays of the weakling sun pierced the morning mist. The taper fell from his fingers and his hand curled into the bear claw of Ullr, a sign to ward off evil.

He shrieked, "Heretic! Heretic! Guards!"

The next instant, they were encompassed in a circle of scarlet flames. The energy field contained their powers efficiently, but could not constrict their movements. Zelia tried to dodge through the wall, pulling Ares behind her, and it moved with them. The adventurer stabbed at the shield as it closed overhead, encasing them in a crimson dome.

No novice, this squirrelly little man in his striped nightdress, Zelia thought, *was set to guard pestilence's door.* She countered with her own spell of crystalline blue, but each thrust and parry she made against the shield only served to shrink it. The orb glowed, drifting and shifting from sapphire to dusky purple, then to dusky burgundy, as though it drew energy from her thrusts.

Again! Fire, like a lightning bolt, shot from her fingers against the encasing shell. Royal blue joined with ruby red and was consumed. The maid was defeated, and the world went whirling away.

Ares dropped his blade and hugged her flaccid form to his chest. The adventurer glared at the glowing circle that surrounded them. Gently, he lowered her to the ground and pulled his war hammer from his belt.

The wizard watched him smugly. Ares swung at the enclosing wall, powering the stroke with his rage. White light sparked from his shoulders down his arms to wrists and hands, arcing between hammer and shield. And then it shattered, with an explosion of many colours.

The sorcerer, little more than an outline obscured by his own shielding, became suddenly clear, and they stared at each other. Shock distorted the little man's features and he blinked at the warrior who had overcome his spell. Ares felt a moment's pity for him. Dwarfed by the giant portal in his flopping gown, with unfastened sandals, the little mage looked ridiculous.

There was the rattle of armour, and the magician's eyes flicked to the far gate. The young elf-man didn't need to look to understand that the Special Police were pouring through the gate behind him. He could not escape that way.

The sorcerer blocked the only other exit, save one. Without a second thought, Ares scooped Zelia from the marble stair and ran, his grey-black cloak snapping out behind him. He slipped between the huge white megaliths and vanished in the Great Circle of the Gods.

Within the Circle of the Nine Astral Planes, the sun of mortal world existed no more. Radiating from the stones were the glowing streaks of the ley-line grid. The brilliant colours drew him towards the circle's heart. And cold. A cold that went beyond the absence of heat, it was a living, breathing thing itself. His marrow froze, and Ares was sure that his hair was going to break off his scalp in so many frozen crystals.

Ares kept walking, vaguely aware as he passed them of the Circle of Seven Planets and its sister circle representing the seven major gods. Then he found himself beside a clear fountain in a quiet glade. The soft greens of spring surrounded him. Wind teased at his hair and kissed his cheek, pausing to flutter over Zelia for a moment before it spiralled and was gone. His feet moved as if from some silent command when his will began to waver. Who knew where, or when, he might end up next?

The ground lurched, as if someone or something had plucked the earth from beneath his feet, propelling him forward. He moved beyond the five pillars of the Moon, the stones smooth and polished, until he stood before the central Stone of Binding. Huge, massive and black, it squatted there, dragging at Ares and his precious burden. He contemplated the single monolith and then thrust himself through the stone, Zelia clenched tightly to his breast.

The next thing he knew he was standing before a woman dressed in funeral white. Her once beautiful features had been sharpened by age and ravaged by disease. He seized at her image. A room coalesced around them. In its centre was a large canopied bed. The woman was stretched on the mattress, clearly in the last throes of death. The adventurer had found the Matriarch at last.

Zelia shrank from the eunuch's baleful stare.

"You! You are the cause of all this." He swung an accusing finger from the shrunken figure of the Matriarch to the maiden. The older woman's stertorous breathing scraped harshly in her chest.

"You and your witchery loosed plague's creatures upon the world. You wanted her to die. She named you successor, and now we discover from her as she lies dying that she names you heir still, heretic though you are. The council meet now to see if they can override her will. You have done this to her, and now," Fidhl spat the words at her, "you come to claim your place."

Ares hissed with a sharp intake of breath and advanced on the eunuch. "If she caused this," Ares indicated the shrivelled form upon the bed, "it was at your mistress's bidding. *She* sent Zelia to find this Queb."

Fidhl paled at the name. "She . . . she couldn't. She wouldn't. The girl was banned."

"Banned but still second, huh?" Ares relaxed, convinced he had made his point. Zelia levered herself from the wall and moved towards the bed, ignoring them both.

"Is it plague?" she asked.

"What else?" Fidhl sniffed at her.

"Ares?"

The warrior swung on her. "What?" he snapped.

"Do you think we can do it?" She nodded at the woman on the bed.

"I don't know. We're both pretty well spent."

"We've got to try. Besides, I think it's a little premature for me to claim my office, don't you? She breathes still, and I have business elsewhere."

"Yes, I suppose you're right. I know *I* have no intention of staying cooped up in this," he scanned the room and then glared at the acolyte, "mausoleum."

The eunuch placed himself between the elfman and the bed.

"Get out of my way, little man, or I may forget this is a holy place." Ares placed a threatening hand on his belt.

Bristling, the eunuch challenged the warrior. "Just what are you going to do?" he croaked, and Zelia had to admire his courage.

"See if we can help her, *if* we're not too tired. Now do you mind?" she said as Ares brushed the acolyte aside.

Zelia sat on the bed, bent her head and placed one hand on the woman's forehead, draping the other over her bony shoulder. Ares sunk down on the opposite side of the bed and mimicked the maid's posture.

"No!" Fidhl's objection echoed dimly as they entered the healing trance. A log popped in the fire, but Ares and Zelia did not hear it. Instead, the sickening swish of blood filled their ears, the swish which would have been a roar if the heart had not been worn beyond reckoning. They smelled the putrescence of death and chased the diabolic presence through narrow arteries. They went deeper, becoming a part of the blood itself, touching all areas of weakness and healing them as they passed in pursuit of plague's demon. The Matriarch's breathing became deeper and more even, without the rasping quality it had had.

Again they approached the fragile light of human spirit and found the fell fiend of pestilence. Zelia poured her energy, and Ares', into the woman's frail body. The subtle illumination of vitality strengthened and flared, and the demon was banished with a shriek. The woman sighed as she moved from coma into a natural sleep, and her colour improved perceptibly. The priestess's eyes fluttered as she descended deeper into sleep. Exhausted, Ares and Zelia stretched out on the bed next to the Matriarch and succumbed to slumber while the astounded acolyte looked on.

Cautiously, Fidhl crept up on the sleeping trio. With a trembling hand, he checked the Matriarch's pulse. Her heartbeat was strong. All traces of the illness were gone. Her skin was cool and dry. He let his hand flit briefly over his mistress's forehead and then yanked it back as though burned. The infection had vanished, and with it the raging fever. His jaw unhinged, his legs gave out from under him, and the eunuch plopped awkwardly into a chair to stare in astonishment at the sleeping pair beside her.

It was all true. They were heretics. Sorcerers.

And they had saved the Matriarch's life, cheating death itself. Fidhl could not find it in his heart to condemn them, so instead he guarded them, keeping watch to make sure all three would slumber undisturbed.

Sun shone brightly through the open windows. A brisk breeze cleared the sickroom of the stale, musty odour of death. Fidhl moved through the room, collecting the accoutrements of treatment to return them to the hospice. When he returned, he carried a tray piled high with food. The Matriarch pointed to the bedside table and nodded her thanks. With a bow, he withdrew.

Leaning against the far wall, Zelia watched him go. "He's a good man. Loyal."

"It's about time you recognized that fact. You have never had much patience with him. You always thought him a trifle stupid. Perhaps I should remind you that it is his loyalty to me that keeps his lips sealed. He, alone of the entire guild, would protect you now. You have not made yourself loved."

"Maybe you too would find the man a bit stupid if every time he looked at you all he saw was a rather chequered ancestry."

"But it is true; you do have unusual ancestry, and it has given you extraordinary powers."

"And see what good it's done me!"

The Matriarch frowned at her and acknowledged Ares with a duck of her head. "Right now I wish I had twenty heretics like the two of you. You saved my life. Tell me, do you think you can teach this skill?"

"I don't think so," Zelia said. "I get the feeling we are fighting something larger than disease. This is no plague borne of rat-infested houses and poor sanitation. This is something else." Her foot tapped impatiently against the ground as she searched for the words to describe the phantom she had encountered. "Besides, it takes both of us. Neither of us can do it alone."

The woman accepted the news with barely a nod. "I'm not surprised; it seems to be beyond our craft."

"And we cannot stay," Zelia continued.

"Yes, I suppose you are right. You must follow Queb. I'm afraid you will find no help here. So, where do you go now?" The Matriarch pulled the tray on to her lap and poked at her food.

Zelia answered for both of them. "South. We think the necromancer's somewhere in Daklha.

All evidence points in that direction. The plague is newly arrived to its shores, and it seems to follow the wizard's path, or perhaps it leads him, but I sense the same sort of disturbance there that once emanated from the north."

"Unfortunately it's a big continent," Ares commented as he swung his chair around to lean against a bedpost. "Personally, I don't relish the idea of traipsing across the four quarters of desert looking for him."

"Perhaps the stick can be made to divulge its secret once we reach Daklha," Zelia said, giving the staff a sharp shake.

"Which reminds me," the high priestess glanced up from the tray. "A message came for you from Shamir."

"A message?"

"Yes, from your stepmother, I believe."

Zelia did a quick double-take. "The Lady Hadidge?"

"Yes, it is over there on the mantel." The Matriarch waved a slice of toasted bread in that direction.

Zelia recognized her stepmother's seal. She picked up the vellum scroll. Curious, Ares strolled over to stand next to her as she unrolled it and scrutinized the cramped writing. Her face clouded as she skimmed its contents.

"I think this simplifies matters." She passed the scroll to Ares, who scanned the scribbled message and rerolled the vellum.

"What simplifies matters?" the Matriarch said, peering at Zelia over the lip of her mug.

"I have no choice in destination now. My father is missing."

"Missing? But he was here."

"Here?"

The Matriarch explained briefly about the sheik's visit. "Does your stepmother say whether or not your father ever returned from his search?"

"No mention of that. She only demands my immediate presence, for it seems whoever abducted my father – and she seems to think it was slavers – is willing to exchange him for ransom, a very specific ransom – me."

"You?" Ares and the priestess chorused.

"Yes, I'm the price for his deliverance. They say they'll exchange my father for me."

The elf-man began to pace up and down the room. "That doesn't make sense. This is no slaver's deal," he said. "No Quattarean would exchange one captive for another, unless there was profit to be made. They certainly wouldn't trade an able-bodied male for a female. No, not even an adventurer would propose such a foolish deal. Where's the profit to be had?

A nobleman, and head of household, for a bastard daughter?"

"Thanks! I needed that," Zelia said.

"You're welcome," he said glibly. "We both know some other hand lies behind this, and I believe we know whose. Yes, I'd say it narrows down our search considerably. Good. I didn't fancy wandering through the four nations of Daklha. I've never been overly fond of sand, unless there's a body of water nearby."

The Matriarch looked incredulously at Ares. "Aren't you concerned?" she asked the elf.

Ares grinned at her. "We're about to go off to a continent that not even the natives seem to love," and his gaze flitted to Zelia, "to do battle with a sorcerer whose form we can't even guess at. *Or . . .*" he paused for effect, "if we prefer, we can stay here and be spitted like a couple of sausages on a stick. Now, what have I got to be worried about?"

Chapter 14

The sun glinted off the deep blue waters, reflecting in brittle diamonds of frolicking light. Ares didn't like it. Even the sea around the Southern Continent of Daklha looked harsh and hard, he thought, as the skiff slipped into the small man-made harbour. Around them the wide coast of Shamir was an acrimonious orange-red glare. In the far distance, he could see the spires of the capital city, Al Khali. Zelia, openly wearing healers' white, stood at the prow squinting at the horizon.

"Looking forward to this family reunion?" Ares leaned against the rail, allowing the salty spray to cool his skin.

Zelia chuffed. "There's little love between my stepmother and myself."

"Why? Because you are illegitimate? That doesn't make sense. I thought multiple wives were the norm in Daklha, so what difference does one more woman make, or child for that matter? How many children does your father have?"

"Dozens – I lose count. No, it's not jealousy or even rivalry. It's because I was a troublemaker. I unsettle her world. I have too much of my mother in me, I suppose. When I was a child I was forever escaping from the terem where I belonged, and when my time came, I refused to take the veil. During one of my escapades, the Emir saw my exposed face and took a fancy to it, hoping to own it and me with it. My rejection was blunt." She made a wry face. "You've never seen the Emir. Woe for the days of old when the Grand Sultan of Shamir was the strongest warrior, rather than the best in husbandry! This particular Emir would never have survived. He's fat and lazy."

The captain's boy scurried fore from aft to inform them of their impending arrival and then scampered away again, a talisman held tightly in his fist. The Matriarch had made sure the captain was well bribed to take on his controversial passengers, but that did little to change their castigation among the damned, and this was reflected in the crew's attitude and behaviour. The captain himself refused to come near them and so the cabin boy did the honours. The brightly scaled Chictaw wing, garish in red, green and gold, was carried as protection against their witchery.

"I could make him a better talisman than that with a bit of twine and some goat's hair," Zelia nodded after the child.

"I'm sure you could," Ares turned back to the crenellated spires of pearl white and cool peach. "Have you given any thought to what we're going to do once we run into our friend Queb?"

"Yes, a lot."

"And?"

"I'm open for suggestions," she quipped.

"Great! Remind me the next time I see a damsel in distress to look the other way."

Swathed from head to toe in black cloth, the Lady Hadidge crouched on the raised dais. Her knees poking against her veil and gown were the only thing that gave her shape, and she looked for all the world like a deadly sand toad perched on a pillow at the head of the table. Ares wiped the sweat from his brow and wondered how the Lady Hadidge could stand the heat, cloaked as she was.

Zelia had warned him, and he had often heard about the terems of Daklha, where the women were kept hidden away. But nothing could have prepared him for this sprawling metropolis of tents which housed the women of Sheik Al Y Kazzam and the eunuchs who tended them. And her father was only a minor dignitary – a member of the lesser nobility. His clan travelled the countryside, coming to the city when summoned or during times of peril.

It was a measure of their need, rather than a measure of the esteem in which they held Zelia, that they permitted him inside the gauzy gates and behind the silken veil more impregnable than any stone fortress of the north. Ares began to understand the impulse which had sent Zelia's freewheeling spirit to the stuffy halls of the healers.

The two women sat facing each other, immovable as stones. Neither blinked, and Ares sensed the conflict of their wills. Finally the older woman shifted.

"You have grown," she said simply.

Zelia accepted her comment with a shrug.

"I am to give this to you." The black lump moved. An arm appeared from between two folds of cloth and beckoned for a slave. The eunuch crawled up to the head of the table, retrieved the folded sheaf from the disembodied hand and then retreated, passing the message to Zelia. She took it and unfolded it, flattening it on her knee. Her eyes widened perceptibly. Her nostrils flared and her jaws clenched, and then she had her features under control again.

Without a word, she handed it to Ares. He glanced briefly at the contents, his eye drawn to the glowing symbol at the bottom which seemed to slither, move and pulsate with a life of its own.

A single letter, a shimmering golden "Q".

Ares and Zelia crested another dune. They had left their strange steeds, the sand snails, far behind. These bizarre creatures replaced the more fragile horses and camels for trips into deep desert beyond oasis and watering hole, help and hope. Although their trip was not that far, the ever-frugal Lady Hadidge refused to give them the faster and more valuable horses. Zelia, it seems, was expendable and the lady did not expect to see her return. When Ares mentioned that the sheik might have need of transport, she had said archly, "He is a Shamir. The desert is his home. He will find his way to us."

Ares contemplated the shimmering trail of slime the snails created as they made their surprisingly speedy path across the sand. It pointed the way home – a home he never hoped to see again. He turned to face the opposite direction. A standing circle of stones had sprouted enigmatically in the middle of nowhere. This was the sacred portal of Shamir, the place where Zelia had been conceived. Behind them, the sheik's camp was lost in the shimmering waves of heat which rippled across the sand. The spirals of the capital city were still visible in the distance, floating like some fairy castle upon ghostly waves that concealed the walls and left the turrets drifting on a cloud of orange and blue.

Ares cursed the climate for the umpteenth time since they had arrived on Shamirian shores. His skin was bright red. He had burned and peeled, burned and peeled. Despite this, he shrugged out of his jerkin and wondered how long it would be before he too turned native and adopted the tent-like garb of the Shamirian.

Zelia trudged behind him, carrying Queb's staff. It seemed to weigh heavily on her spirit. The nearer they drew to their goal, the more her pace slowed, as though the stick were dragging her down, pulling her closer and closer to the earth. She clambered through the shifting sands to stay abreast of Ares.

The ruddy standing stones sprang like grinning, jagged teeth from the ground. This circle gave Ares a feeling of foreboding that he had never felt in Szatmar or Thessalia. He shivered despite the heat and turned to wait for Zelia, unwilling to gaze at the stones.

Panting, Zelia struggled up beside him and gave him a wan smile. "So it seems that we have come from pole to pole, you and I. From the Wastes where you found your beginning to here where I found mine."

The adventurer made a rude noise. "Next trip, why don't we go somewhere different? Somewhere neither of us have ever been before?"

Side by side, they examined the circle. Ares cleared his throat. Then they faced each other. Her eyes stared deep into his as if to plead with him to stay behind. Ares realized that she still considered this to be her battle alone, now more than ever since her father was held captive, and he knew that she did not expect to see another dawn.

Saying nothing, he took her hand. "Ready?"

With a sigh, she relented. As one, they stepped into the shadow of one of the stones. The temperature plummeted. *Og, it was cold!*

Chapter 15

Astra Aurelius sat before the cool fountain in the standing circle of stones. Ephemeral as her cousins the will o' wisps, the air elemental could only be glimpsed out of the corner of a mortal eye and could be seen only as a ripple in the human consciousness.

The nymph liked this spot. In some other place, some otherwhen, this was a desert, arid and dry, a place little visited by her sister spirits, the water elementals. It had been in that other world that she met the human male whose black hair and even blacker eye had so captivated her heart. So captivated her heart that she had forgotten her responsibilities, losing that which had been placed in her charge.

The Lady Astra frowned and waved the unpleasant thought away.

The man had been pretty and here, beside this fountain, they had performed the sacred union. From that union had come a child, but the gods had punished her for her lapse, making the babe more human than fairy. Thus the child had size and mass, and Astra had done what the gods – and necessity – demanded of her and had given the babe over to her sire. She had done it unwillingly, for she loved her daughter with as much steadfastness as was available to a creature of the wind. Often the nymph wondered what had become of her daughter, and then she would come here to the place where the girl had been conceived.

Somewhere a bird trilled, and the airy elemental lost the thought. Like so many thoughts, it was tossed aside with the first gentle breeze. Blue hair as light as gossamer floated around her head in a fairy nimbus, shifting continually as though lifted by a stirring wind that none other felt.

Something, someone, moved between worlds, between time, and . . . something about the touch seemed familiar. The elemental glanced up, yearning after its fleeting caress.

The nebulous form wavered and dissipated

a breathy puff, and before she knew it the lady was being drawn, stretched as thin as a single silken thread, by the disturbance through the portals between the worlds.

Around them, the small tidy stones of Shamir had been replaced by a colossus in black stones. Beyond them, parched earth the colour of clay spread as far as the eye could see. The Miasmic Swamp of Abdha belied its name. This far northwestern portion of Daklha was one of the few which regularly saw rain, and the land was subject to an annual flood, but the waters soon receded and the ground was riddled with fissures. The dried mud curled and writhed under a baking sun. The floods had weakened their structure, undermining the stones, and they stood at odd angles, canting this way and that.

The rains were no gift to the swamp that was no swamp, for their waters were contaminated by the soil itself, and this deadly combination of noxious soil and fouled water ensured that nothing lived here save Apsu's Coat, named after the great lizard god of Abdha. Thought to be his sloughing skin, the trees had thick bark with overlapping scales that could easily have graced Brimstone's dragons. Their annual growth thwarted by flood, the trees were small. Their branches bent low, wilting under the weight of the oppressive heat. Long tendrils snaked across the ground in search of moisture. These twisting limbs were covered with huge thorns, which swelled and blossomed into sickening bulbous growths that popped as Ares watched. The vegetation sloughed a thick black sludge of spores that fell to the writhing floor with a faint plop and tainted the air with a vile stench.

Looking around, Ares decided he actually liked the desert after all and wished himself away. He took a tentative step forward, and a snaking vine wrapped itself around his ankle. Another lashed out and grabbed his wrist before he had the chance to remove his sword from its scabbard.

Zelia sidled closer to her companion, establishing contact just as Queb materialized above their heads. Or at least what remained of him became visible.

The fell visage shifted continuously as though the wizard had difficulty maintaining even the memory of human shape and form. An arm appeared in the roiling cloud here, then a leg. Lips, a mouth and a nose surfaced from the depths of the whirlwind and rearranged themselves. The two eyes moved into more or less a straight line. The nose settled, slightly askew, below the eyes, and the mouth below the nose, forming an approximation of a human face. The lips grew to enormous size, and the mouth opened slowly to disgorge Zelia's father.

The sheik collapsed, bound and gagged, folding like an empty cloak on the hardened earth below the swirling apparition. The open mouth screeched a deafening challenge. Again the billowing form tried to attain human semblance. An image of the ancient archmage appeared, only to dissolve into a spinning ball of miscellaneous parts.

Then the image hardened, as if the necromancer had reached a crucial decision. It solidified not into the shape of a man, but into the shape of Brimstone's dragon. It rose screaming into the sky and swooped, spitting fire. Ares was held pinioned by the vines, and Zelia again wondered what lunacy had led her here. She tried to think, rifling through her cluttered mind for the words of a spell to banish the beast, but her mind froze. Any and all wizardry she had ever known flew from the plunging, shrieking creature. Closer and closer it zoomed, filling the horizon, and she shrank into Ares' loosely bound arms. Then she felt a chill as the image passed *through* them. It soared, changing to form the giant hammer of Og, but when it descended she didn't flinch.

"He can't hurt us!" Ares shouted triumphantly. "He has no physical form."

"Don't get cocky," she said, seizing Ares' arm and shaking it. "He toys with us as a cat does a mouse." A spell flew to Zelia's lips and the bonds which held Ares crumpled into dust and they were engulfed in a blast of powder which Ares deflected as he had once deflected the falling detritus of a mountain. Only this time, he was aware he was doing it. A look of amazement skittered across his face, followed by consternation. The shield faded and then blazed.

Queb turned his attack towards the white-haired figure, and the glowing bubble was beaten steadily back until its tent-like top was pressed against his features, and they showed through, startled and white. Ares began to squirm like a fish on a hook, his eyes bulging from his head. His fingers went to his throat, and beneath this pale shroud, his sun-reddened skin turned an even angrier purple. He choked and gagged.

Something slipped within Zelia's mind, tinging all her thoughts the bright red of rage. She shrieked a counterspell. The shield vanished, as did the power which attempted to crush it. Ares sagged against her, suddenly able to breathe again. He gasped for air.

Lips formed again in the billowing cloud. "I can make things most unpleasant for you and for those you love, fairy whelp!"

With that, her father began to dance around like a marionette on a string, leaping, twisting and turning, his body contorting into any number of impossible positions. She was sure that his back would break. Blood roared past her temples. Something, like a sleepy summer fly, buzzed next to her ear and Zelia found within herself a power source that she didn't know she possessed. Lightning flashed from her fingertips, sizzling directly into the centre of the roiling cloud. The spinning mist dimmed, muddying.

Ares' gaze was drawn away from the swirling wizard and spinning sheik, for he thought he had seen . . . something . . . flitting through the stone circle. He scanned the bleak environment and saw nothing.

Zelia unleashed another bolt, and it fragmented only to reform. Occasionally faces would surface from the cloud, faces of those she loved writhing in agony.

Again! And the cloud simply dispersed, sundering only to unite in a new configuration of lips, eye, arm and thigh.

Flashes of light and colour bounced around the stone circle in a dazzling array. Back and forth, to and fro, and she attacked and was battered back again, unable to overcome this enemy which could simply dissipate against each new onslaught only to reform, the energy absorbed and redirected at her.

There was a flicker of movement from somewhere behind her, and Zelia felt warmth as Ares placed a tremulous hand on her shoulder, adding his power to her own. Reds, yellows, blues reflected against the ochre sky where even the sun had hidden from their onslaught. A wind ripped around them, grabbing Zelia's robes and tearing at them.

The wizard met each thrust without resistance. The nightmare image of twitching human parts splintered, scattered and congealed again. Shrieking laughter rebounded throughout the circle while her father continued his joggling, jerking dance, airborne.

Something tickled in Ares' ear, and the power that he poured into Zelia surged back again, amplified. Their spirits mingled, entwining until they became one, and there was no limit to their power. They shed the shackles of their bodies and sent their combined spirit to interpose itself between the sheik and the necromancer's spell. Her father plummeted while their bodies began to do a twitching jig on the ground as the wizard turned his wrath against the unhoused shells.

This spirit that was neither Ares nor Zelia but the two of them as one reached out along the ley-lines, exploring far away.

Reaching beyond the circle, they gathered the many strands of magic. Using the power circles, Ares-Zelia/Zelia-Ares moved from portal to poral, collecting sorcery everywhere they went. The magic of an old witch woman's simple, the young girl's potion of love or the scrying of maids in water, the wizardry of the lone court magician – all were brought into their weaving. The Matriarch felt their touch and merged with them joyfully, bringing the clerics of Brigitta with her, and the sisters augmented the couple's power with the sorcery of healing. Still Ares-Zelia cast about, searching for more.

The unseen Queb appeared, tied to this circle of stone, as if his magic were linked to a power that came from another, darker source, that bound him here, for he did not follow. Instead, the wizard raged futilely, unable to pursue their fleeing spirit along the ley.

Their united essence shot beyond the Northern Wastes where they met Ares' mirror image, his brethren the snow elves, who added their chill magic to his. Then they seized the wizardry of the berserkers as they danced Og's sacred dance in worship of their bloody god. They sought out the talent of the sleeping latent in village, field and farm and grasped it.

Last they went spiralling south, where they

hovered over the Isle of Pelopnos. Descending, they gathered the myriad enchantments of apprentice and journeyman – the schoolboy's prank and the master's learned demonstration – and wrested it for their use. They were blasted with a roar of protest as the masters tried to resist, and then someone else was looking through their human eyes at the churning image of Queb. The Inquisitor railed about blasphemy while the Archmage quailed before the image of Queb reborn, but in the end they relented, and the wizards' power was theirs to command.

Something tingled throughout their collective consciousness, and two words echoed in their unified mind: "My daughter."

A second whirlwind blew around the circle. It seemed to embrace the spinning mage. Faster and faster it spun, matching its speed to that of the necromancer and squeezing the wizard. Faster and faster and faster it blew, rotating on an ever smaller axis. The wizard's image coalesced, becoming vaguely recognizable, gaining form and shape and eventually solidity and mass.

The wizard's words buzzed in their minds: "You! YOU!"

And then Ares-Zelia felt no more, for they had become receptacles through which flowed all the magic from this world and the many other worlds. And they no longer stood among trees contorted into fantastical shapes, snaking under a scorched sky, but in a grassy green glen near a whispering fountain under a pale pink sun. Then they flew between the planes, no longer possessors of this otherworld magic but possessed by it. They had glimpses of fire and brimstone, night and death, strange gods.

The energy of the nine planes funnelled through the two of them, linked as they were, and on the ground two pairs of arms were raised from slumping bodies to point at the roiling necromancer trapped inside the twirling cyclone made of an infinite number of tiny flickering figures. This external maelstrom flowed past the necromancer, shrinking until he was compressed into a nice tiny knot, smaller than his human form, smaller than a child, smaller even than a mouse. A mouth escaped from the side. Two lips opened wide, screaming.

A rising current rippled through them as they channelled the gathered power at the seething whirlwind, enveloping it in a blinding blast. The cyclone exploded. Hades' demons and imps fled, and the spirit that had once been the necromancer Queb was left unprotected at last as Satan released his savage hold on the wizard's soul. It shattered into a million tiny shards. The staff, still cradled in Zelia's arm, splintered, and Ares felt phantom pain as the splinters were driven into his flesh somewhere on the other side of the circle.

The air around them sizzled and popped and the circle was peopled by the same tiny figures that had appeared so fleetingly in the maelstrom. Only subliminally seen, they had fragile faces with sharp, fay features that softened and wavered as they moved. Chattering, they flitted around the clearing in diaphanous blue, carrying with them a breath of fresh air.

For a moment they were surrounded by a thousand flickering entities that chittered and cheered. Their names were spoken in voices like wind sloughing through tall grass, and then these tiny beings plucked the many atoms and molecules that had been Queb's and vanished, each taking a piece of the sundered consciousness with them. The area was cleared, and the thing that had once been the necromancer was scattered to the four corners of this mortal world and the nine planes, spread throughout the worlds and between them. And Queb was nothing more than a random strand of thought and fragmented consciousness.

The wind dropped as quickly as it had come. The air was still and dry. The silence wrapped around them and they were loosed from their thrall. Hands entwined as they were sucked into their bodies.

Ares and Zelia stood alone in the small antechamber beyond the Great Chapel, awaiting the ceremony. A bard chanted a stylized poem of their heroics, which left Zelia blushing. Perhaps raising them to superhuman status made her and Ares' success more palatable to the wizards, but Zelia wished they'd get on with it.

The censer swung, and smoke hung suspended in the stale air. The Archmage and Grand Inquisitor looked as uncomfortable as she felt. Zelia scratched her neck and shifted nervously from one foot to another. Ares grinned wickedly at her and picked at the loose thread that tickled her neck. He rolled his eyes to the heavens and then plucked at his own gown, pulling it away from his throat.

In the velvet blue robes of a master sorcerer, Zelia felt decked out like a scarecrow. The cloth was made rigid with the many gold embroidered symbols. Even her bells of office chiming softly about her neck seemed weighted – a responsibility too heavy to bear. Why had she wanted to return to *this?* Zelia wondered.

The chant changed in cadence, and many voices joined the one in issuing the invitation to join them in their sacred realm. The young couple took a measured step forward, and then another, as the persuasive voice of the college choir urged them on. Smoke eddied about them. A sneeze tickled Zelia's nose and she twitched it, ticking off the number of steps on her fingers – one each for the many gods, the planets, the moons and the planes – until they reached the great altar.

With a flourish, the Archmage handed them their staffs, hers topped with a sapphire and his with a clear white crystal. The Grand Inquisitor presented them their diplomas as Master Wizards Emeritus.

Zelia caught Ares' soft snigger and only barely managed to keep a straight face herself.

The Archmage raised his hand in the four-fingered sign of benediction just as Ares clasped her hand, a question in his ice-blue eyes.

They looked at each other, his impish grin reflected on her own features, and Zelia nodded. The wizards' voices faltered and their song of welcome waned to a single tremulous note as the two vanished from the great hall.

They reappeared in a world of subtle green, in some otherwhen, as though drawn there. Giddy with relief, they collapsed laughing beside the sparkling fountain as a gentle breeze rattled around them, brushing Ares' cheek like a tender caress.

The adventurer-cum-wizard saw something flash in the corner of his eye – a flickering impression that disappeared when faced fully. It was a beautiful blue maiden who could easily have been Zelia's twin only smaller, more delicate. The image wavered, solidified, wavered again and then coalesced as if it were etched in smoke that was blown about in misty tatters by the faintest whisper of a breeze.

A voice spoke, sounding like the rustle of autumn leaves in the blustering wind. It rattled inside his skull. The words brought an unaccustomed mist to his eyes as he gazed sidelong at the long-abandoned and forgotten daughter.

It said: "Welcome, daughter. I've been wanting to meet you for a long time."

Tears sprang to Zelia's eyes and she reached out for her mother. The elemental danced lightly away, evading her grasp.

"And you," the form swooped to dart around Ares' head, "there's someone awaiting you also," she buzzed.

The scene around them melted and then solidified into snow-white crystals, and the couple found themselves shivering in a palace of ice, looking out on an island surrounded by an ocean of mists.

And the adventures of Zelia and Ares continue in The Fire Wars.

APPENDIX
The Renegades World and its People

The universe

The Renegades' universe is viewed laterally rather than spatially. Thus, what we would call "parallel universes" are considered part and parcel of a single universe. We think in three dimensions, therefore our universe includes the heavens above. However, the citizen of Renegades World tends to reason sideways (probably one of the reasons why there is so little progress), which means that the sky above as seen in the Earth plane is only the mortal sky. The sky in the adjacent plane is different, although some of the constellations may be similar.

Because of this sidewise thinking, primitive man used to view the universe as flat. This hypothesis has largely been dismissed as folly. More modern theories have replaced it to allow for at least some vertical movement. The more popular include the Concept of the Eternal Ice Cream Cone and the Onion Theory. The former likens the nine planes to an ice cream cone with the most compressed and most dense earth pushed to the bottom, and the more expansive and broader planes piled on top of it. This concept has been discredited since most people would agree that ice cream is a bad medium for binding a universe together. Of the two, the Onion Theory is the more recent and widely accepted by the scientific community as being true. It was formulated by Sir Ph'ig Nu'ton, noted physicist, after he was hit on the head by a flying pumpkin at a football match.[1] This caused a pretty nasty concussion and a random inspired thought, whereupon he decided that the universe resembled an onion which could be peeled layer by layer to reveal the next layer or plane.

There are nine planes, which are noted as follows. The first four are the elemental planes:

1. In Renegades World, pumpkins, melons and other such vegetable matter are used instead of balls. This is supposed to add zest to the game.

Earth, Air, Water and Fire. The next two are called the Planes of Death, and the last three are known collectively as the Planes of Immortality.

The inner plane belongs to the earth elementals. However, they became so enamoured of the earth that eventually they became a part of that which they ruled, incidentally creating a friendly habitat for man. True earth elementals are difficult to come by now, although they may be found in the other planes. They are by nature inflexible, with a memory as long and as old as the earth itself, and the only elementals to have some concept of time.

The second plane belongs to Air. It acts as a buffer between the Earth and Water planes. Thus, air elementals have inadvertently become protectors of humankind, guarding them against waters' deluge. The next plane is Water's realm. It too acts as a buffer between the Air plane and the following plane, belonging to Fire. These two elements are prone to disputes. Air loves to whip fire into a frenzy while fire always leaps into air, invading its space. The fourth and final of the elemental planes belongs to Fire. It is called the Brimstone realm by mortal man. Here are found dragons, salamanders and other of flame's creatures.

The next two are the Planes of Death (although the Brimstone realm is sometimes included in this category). The first (or the fifth, depending on the way you choose to count the planes) is the Plane of Night. It is a place of fell magic where wampyrs and werebeasts in all forms reside. It is home to incubi and succubi. This is a plane of lost souls and, according to the wizards, it is reputed to be the place where witches come after death. The sixth plane is Hades, equivalent to our hell. It is the dominion of devils and demons, and the place where sinners – heretics and suchlike – come after death.

The final three planes are the Realm of Immortality, although this is not a completely accurate description, since elementals are also immortal. The seventh plane is Day's domain, the nearest equivalent to our heaven. It is often referred to as the Dream Fields. This is where the good come to live out eternity. It is a place of daemons and angels. The eighth is the home of gods, and here all the gods, godlings, goddesses and their minions, past and present, are said to abide.

In the final plane dwell beings so different, so incomprehensible to mortal mind, that they have no name. They are pure ethereal beings, or being. (There is some debate as to whether or not there are more than one of these creatures. Some scientists, usually Ice Creamists, contend that the final plane is in fact one rather large, cold and very fluffy being, but all agree that it(they) is(are) thing(s) of spirit.) This plane, also sometimes called the nether world, is the final ring that binds and holds all the others together.

The planes intersect with mortal lands at sacred portals. Such places are usually marked by giant circles of stones, similar to Stonehenge. It is believed that those constellations, common to all planes, are celestial doorways, just as the stone circles are portals upon the land masses.

The luminaries (the sun and the moons)

There are a total of six luminaries, including both the sun and the moons. All together the luminaries emit the six colours of healing. Orange is the colour of the sun, while each moon's radiance is tinted with the colours – red, yellow, blue, green and purple – from which come their names. When mixed, their colours make the pure white light that is the primary colour of healing and healers.

The moons are said to be the five daughters of Brigitta. (She has only one son.) They are exact duplicates of herself, cast off as a defence (and in the hope that at least one of herself would survive) during the rape by the war god Og, from which the godling Ares sprung. The five moons seldom appear in the sky all at one time. It seems the sisters quarrel constantly, arguing over whose errant husband the sun truly is. Therefore, the Renegades' sun doesn't set so much as hide from the relentless pursuit of the five amorous moons.

The planets

Like the gods, there are seven of them (excluding the sun, which is considered a luminary rather than a planet). The planets are named after the gods and goddesses who supposedly have rulership over them. Therefore, the names of the planets change from country to country as the names of the gods change. Furthermore, which god has rulership over what planet, along with their respective attributes, may miraculously transform as soon as the weary traveller crosses the border. The largest planet, deemed the most important, is named accordingly, dependent upon which god or goddess has pre-eminence in a given country. The fact that the largest planet may be called Fennec in one country (and be considered a sneak and a thief) and Og (an adventurer and berserker) in another is a great cause of confusion and consternation at science conferences, and has been the cause of several holy wars. The science of astrology has fallen into disrepute for this reason.

The gods

Each country has a god, goddess or multiple godlings. Sometimes neighbouring countries will share deities. Each profession claims a patron. Like pre-Christian earth, gods and their related hierarchies come and go, gaining in importance or sinking into oblivion as societies change and evolve. This has resulted in enough gods and goddesses to fill not only a volume but an entire library, which they do.[2]

The gods themselves reside in the eighth plane. Needless to say, this plane is a bit congested, making the gods a trifle peevish at the best of times, and people go to great lengths to appease them. In truth, though, many gods and goddesses are usually too caught up with their own internal disputes – usually involving real estate – to interfere with man. However, it is better not to attract a particular god's attention, especially by dabbling in what they would consider their particular area of expertise.

A further consequence of this continuous

2. The library is located, appropriately enough, on Godliness Boulevard in Thessalia, which not surprisingly runs parallel to Cleanliness Avenue, the road of washerwomen.

evolution of the gods/goddesses is that Renegades World can boast some bizarre divinities. One former god, god of bureaucrats, was worshipped with enormous quantities of red tape. Under the unlikely title of Xdizqtojaljluhtkdlfaut – bureaucrats preferring not to be understood – this god reputedly had the head of a stoat, the body of a gerbil, the wings of a dodo, the legs of a chicken and the brain of a pea. Others were worse, a horrific miscellany of churning parts. As man has become more sophisticated, his gods have become more tidy.

Current gods/goddesses include:

Og

The Iron god, whose symbol is the hammer. A warlike god, he is worshipped in the far north, common to both Norvon and Szatmar. He is the patron of berserkers, and vicariously of adventurers and mercenaries. Therefore, his worshippers may be found anywhere such people go, even in Daklha. Og is believed to imbue his followers with fanatical strength and courage, and few who have faced them in conflict would argue the point, which would most likely be at the end of a dagger.

Ullr

The Bear god, is the primary god of Uri, but the bear is also worshipped in the southern regions of Norvon. Less savage than Og, he is the god of perseverance and strength. His followers, who trust in his strength, believe all will eventually find the true god and do not seek converts, as Oggites do, at the end of a knife. A severed bear's paw is supposed to have curative powers, relieving pain and healing piles.

Fennec

The Fox is the god of craft, cunning and, to a lesser extent, deceit. He is worshipped in Firth where such traits are considered laudable. In the northern continent, Fennec is believed to be the patron of all merchants and of thieves.

Brigitta

The only major Northern goddess, her name is pronounced with a soft "g" sound. Her symbol is the dove or a single sheaf of wheat. She is goddess of peace and fecundity and the mother of the moons. She is mainly worshipped in Shalop and northern Lavanthia. She is patroness of the healers' craft.

Apsu

The Devourer and Serpent King, is worshipped in Quattara and the regions around the Miasmic Swamp of Abdha. Accepted patron of all slavers, and indigestion, Apsu is believed by many to be a god of inherent evil. Thus, to a lesser extent, he is the patron of assassins, usurers, insurance salesmen and used-dung-camel dealers.

Sala
The female manifestation (and wife) of Apsu, is worshipped in Abdha and Hamadan. Her symbol is the snake devouring its tail. Neither good nor evil, she is neutral. She claims rulership over all cycles, hence she rules the annual floods and the movement of the planets.

Ramman
The formless one, is the primary god of Shamir and a secondary god in Hamadan. The formless one's name must not be spoken. Blasphemers have their tongues cut out for the first offence (and following such punishment there never is a second one). Quattareans, with typical disrespect, often use the name – their favourite oath being "By Ramman's beard!"

Additional minor deities are worshipped in the various regions. Often these are the offspring of other gods, such as Ares, son of Og and Brigitta. They are referred to as godlings. Where magic is strong, especially near the stone circles, elementals are held sacred. Often deities vie for supremacy and "religious conflict" is common. Of all the crafts, only the wizards reject the concept of a patron deity. Believing they are "above that sort of thing", they claim all gods as their own.

Elementals

Generally speaking, the true elementals, or fairy folk, remain in their corresponding planes. As noted previously, the first plane is attributed to Earth. Being the most dense, it is the most hospitable to man. Earth elementals are strange, rock-like creatures that come in all sizes and shapes. They blend easily into the background and move so slowly that they usually can't be distinguished from their environment.[3] Like Earth, Air, Water and Fire reflect their elements. Fire appears as flames in almost human form, with two arms and two legs and a feverish head. They expand and contract according to mood, becoming small and slightly bluish when they are content, and larger and red-hot when they are angry. They scorch whatever they touch. Air elementals are the intellectuals of the fairy folk. Representing pure thought, without practical applications, they are inclined

3. The old fable of the Slug and the Earth Elemental contains more than a metaphorical grain of truth. This tale relates how the slug had travelled halfway around the circumference of the Earth plane before the earth elemental could lift a lumpy, lithologic leg.

to be flighty and have a poor memory. To humans, air elementals look like smoke upon the breeze. Water is only slightly more stable (and a lot wetter) than either of the other two groups. Emotional creatures, water elementals get extremely bubbly and effervescent when they are happy, and weepy when sad.

Elementals have the ability to travel between planes – a trip normally fatal for man – and occasionally they create havoc in the mortal realm. The appearance of an elemental can be disorienting for a human since their physical presence distorts the mortal time-frame continuum of past, present and future.

True elementals, or fairy folk, should not be confused with elves or any other of their descendants on mortal earth. As noted, fairy folk are made up of the element which they represent and, in the planes beyond the first one, could best be described as two dimensional (or that would be the nearest human equivalent). It is this two-dimensional quality of the other planes that makes interplaner trips lethal for man. Furthermore, it is this 2D-effect that causes disturbances in mortal time.

Fairy folk would most likely appear flat to a human, if they choose to appear at all. They can become three dimensional, blowing up like a balloon, but this requires the expenditure of a great deal of energy. Furthermore, in attaining mass – or, in this case, volume – they tend to lose substance. Due to its unique qualities, it is only on the Earth plane that they can attain true mass, having three dimensions and being quite solid. This, though, is a matter of personal choice. However, they usually consider the whole procedure much too bothersome just to appear more "normal" to mortals.

As a group, elementals are little understood. In modern times, they tend to avoid contact with man. Mixing with elementals can be hazardous to human health, and those they touch – assuming the hapless human survives – remain forever changed, making them "different" from the rest of mankind.

The mortal plane

The Earth plane is a place without toilets and other social amenities. Peasant and nobles alike sleep in a common bed, sharing it with other members of the family, the family livestock and no few fleas. A small, elite group of nobility govern a large peasant base and an even smaller merchant class, and guilds dominate all other aspects of human existence.

Death is a constant companion, while magic which leaks in from the other planes is alive and well – if a little unruly – and human belief in it is strong. Like everything else, the use of sorcery is tightly regulated by the Wizards' Guild. It is taught only to the talented and this talent is thought to be hereditary. Talent is considered exclusively a male trait, often associated with a big nose, weak eyes and (for some unknown reason) a small bladder. Apt apprentices must first have attended an approved preparatory school, and to gain entry into the college, the student must be sponsored by a member of the craft. In practical terms this means that potential pupils are restricted to family members of the guild or those nobles or merchants who have sufficient gold coin to bribe a guild member.

Master wizards are employed by courts, but occasional "freelancers" will work for political causes or hire out to guilds. Access to skilled wizards and wizardry itself are denied to the poor. However, most villages have their witches who, despite prohibition, are mainly females. The village witch is held in high esteem. These women are the doctors, the lawyers, the midwives, the marriage brokers – and sometime plumbers – for their community. They say they can cure anything from the common cold to warts, claims that not even the healers make. If caught practising their craft, they are tried by the Wizards' Guild, a messy process usually involving pins, hot pokers and other instruments of torture. If convicted – and, once tried, few are not convicted – witches are burned at the stake. Because village witches are a valuable commodity the peasants protect them, hiding them from the prying eyes of the gentry and any itinerant guildsman who happen to come along to investigate a magical disturbance.

Generally the position of women is poor. On both continents women are property, owned first by their fathers and then by their spouses, and there is a lively slave trade in little girls even outside the slaver state of Quattara. Independence is a trait which is frowned upon, and any woman who lives alone is immediately suspected of witchcraft. Polygamy is common on the southern continent of Daklha, where women are segregated into terems. In all countries save Shalop their legal rights are nil. They cannot own or inherit land. If wronged, a woman cannot bring the perpetrator to justice. Instead, they must rely on their male relatives' desire to seek vengeance, usually dependent on whether the woman in question was permanently scarred which would decrease her market value.

Only in one area do women reign supreme – the healers' craft, such being considered a suitable occupation for a woman. (Most wizards vanish at the merest whisper of a contagion.) Those men who join the profession must give up their "manhood" and become eunuchs in order to protect the purity of the other initiates. Predictably, male healers are rare.

Like pre-Arthurian England, the fairy folk, little people, elves, dwarves, etc. still exist. It is believed that in times past Earth's realm was open to all true elementals or fairy folk, but as man's population swelled the doors between the planes closed and only a few elementals chose to remain. Through the aeons that followed, their long-term descendants were irrevocably altered by their environment, achieving mortal mass and becoming mortal also, albeit long-lived. These are the trolls, the goblins, pixies and dwarves (earth elementals), and the many different kinds of elves (air and water). Only the fire elementals, harmful to man by their very nature, are not represented by descendants on the mortal plane, although the explosive (and usually red-haired) Firthian is said to have been touched by flame, and the jinn of the southern continent is said to have a fiery temper.

With few exceptions, dwarves, elves and such-like keep to themselves. The little people, brownies and pixies, have their adoptive families. The trolls guard their individual bridges and consume human flesh. The different groups usually stay in their separate enclaves. Goblins and dwarves inhabit the mountainous region in the north. The goblins make occasional forays into human settlements to harvest the more tender women and children, who will be taken to live in their caves and kept like cattle awaiting slaughter. The elves maintain their cities: sea elves along the Shalop coast, snow elves beyond the northern wastes, wood elves in the foothills of the mountains. For most part, their presence is never felt. Their influence wanes and their homes are protected from human incursion by magic.

The jinn is unique to the southern continent of Daklha. Some say it is the fire's scion since it is only able to survive in the arid desert, and it lives, quite notably, in lamps. Totally irascible, it is a point of interest that none of the elementals, even the fire elementals, are willing to claim the jinn as one of their own.

Geographical information

The Island of Pelopnos

This lies more or less between the two major continents. Although it is located slightly east of both, it is still called the Centre of the Universe. It is the citadel and font of all knowledge and is therefore also known as the Isle of Learning because most of the major colleges are found there. These include the Wizards' College, the Healers' College and the minor schools of the Theatre and Minstrel Guilds, along with the other guild schools of lesser artistry and sophistry. Preparatory schools, particularly for wizardry, are located elsewhere, the population of the capital city of Thessalia having grown quite tired of waking up else in someone else's body or someone else's bed in the aftermath of a junior student's spell. The most powerful of all the stone circles is located on Pelopnos.

Eubonia

The northern continent is the larger of the two. A mountain chain divides east and west and the seven countries of Eubonia fall to either side of this chain. The mountains themselves form a sort of no-man's-land where goblins, dwarves, and wood elves dwell.

Ticino is located in the southeast corner, and would be comparable to Italy. Closest to the Blessed Isle, it is the most civilized and is composed entirely of small, nearly independent city-states. Its population is largely mercantile. Directly north of Ticino lies *Uri*, similar to Germany in both culture and social structure. A lesser circle is found here, and the seers of Ullr, the national deity, maintain a temple near the circle. Above that is *Norvon* with its capital city of Bosnos. Along the border of *Norvon* and *Szatmar* lies the Northern Wastes – a vast tundra. The primary circle of the northern continent, destroyed during the battle with Queb, is located in the Wastes. North of the Wastes lies the peninsula-kingdom of *Szatmar.* It is connected to the main continent by the narrowest band of land no more than a kilometre across and is therefore separated physically, politically and socially. The people are primitive and warlike – berserkers who make forays into the civilized countries for plunder and slaves. It is rumoured that they are human descendants of goblins.

West of Szatmar is the country of *Firth*. It is a rugged, wild country, mainly composed of highlands. The people are divided into clans which are nearly autonomous. While there is a hereditary king, he is weak, and as often as not stays in hiding. His life is forfeit if, during one of the numerous petty feuds that periodically rock the kingdom, it is decided that his death would be politically expedient. Therefore the average king's life expectancy is zero, and he tends not to call attention to himself by doing anything inconvenient like ruling. Many of those who have suddenly discovered themselves in line for the throne after the untimely demise of a predecessor have found it advisable to remove themselves to a healthier climate, preferrably somewhere on the southern continent.

South of Firth lies *Shalop*. Because it is the only Northern country to worship a female god, the women of *Shalop* are in a slightly better legal position. For example, they can inherit land and head households, even rule, but only when there is no direct male heir. Hence Shalop is the only country to have a queen. The sea elves live along the coast, carefully cloaked and veiled by magical mists. The second largest stone circle on the continent is located on the southern border and, like the circle of the Wastes, marks the dividing line between two countries.

Shalop's nearest neighbour is *Lavanthia* which lies on the southwest corner of the continent. Lavanthia is rural and its people agrarian. The only two cities of note are elfin and these are hidden by fog. Shalop and Lavanthia boast the largest population of little people, brownies and pixies, and for this reason they are considered blessed, a reputation that is more than earned. Of all the northern continent, they are the most stable politically and are peaceful neighbours. Conflict is limited to quibbling over which of the two sovereigns will take precedence during the annual Brigitta Day parade, which they celebrate jointly at the stone circle along their common border.

Daklha

The southern continent is the smaller of the two and is divided evenly into four countries. Except for the far northwest corner, it is mainly desert. Subject to torrential rains in the spring, this portion is covered in dense jungle (made up primarily of Apsu's Coat) that dries up to skeletal remains during the long dry seasons. Known as the Miasmic Swamp, it is located in the country *Abdha*. Its people, like most of the inhabitants of Daklha, are nomad. The jungle is regarded with suspicion and is considered a source of great evil. A lesser circle is found here. The land itself is tainted, and those few people who have tried to settle there usually contract a rotting disease similar to leprosy, for which there is no known cure.

Due east of Abdha is *Hamadan*. It is doubly and triply blessed. Thanks to the rains of Abdha, a large river runs a winding course through Hamadan from west to east. Like the Nile it floods annually. Though the water is tainted at the source, it is filtered and purified by the limestone and sand over which it must pass on its way to the eastern seaboard. Because of its proximity to Pelopnos, Hamadan is considered the most refined country on the southern continent. Its engineers are unsurpassed in all the known world. Thus, Hamadan has developed an extensive irrigation system which allows the people to cultivate a vast territory, transforming the entire country into something of an oasis.

Shamir in the southeast is desert and its people nomadic. The largest stone circle on the southern continent lies next to the busy seaside port and capital city. The Emir, from his palace in Al Khali, maintains strict control over the tribal sheiks, their offspring and their produce. The Shamir are renowned throughout the mortal plane for their excellent horses, which are sought the world over. It is said the Shamirian cannot be separated from his horse. Aside from his distinctive horsey aroma, a Shamirian can usually be spotted by the straw in his hair. Even the governorship of the country is dependent on horses. Upon the death of the current Emir a race is held. The sheik whose stock (each family is permitted to enter one horse) wins the race becomes the next ruler.

The remaining country is *Quattara*, located in the southwest corner. It has none of the unique land features or redeeming characteristics of its neighbours. A savage place, the slave trade flourishes here. Indeed, it is the only thing that flourishes besides warfare, for the many petty sheiks and sultans are constantly waging war between each other or invading their neighbouring countries in order to renew their one and only resource – slaves. The Quattareans, like the wizards, are known for their bad taste (often attributed to colour-blindness). The phrase "tackier that a Quattarean's tent" reflects this, and the Quattarean can easily be recognized by the gold rings he (or she) wears, adorning each finger, arm, ankle and wrist, and piercing nose, ears and lips.

In and amongst these major countries are numerous duchies and minor principalities, which are usually isolated by geographic location, such as the plateau principality of *Merovnick*. There are islands scattered around both continents and each contains their own petty kingdom and reigning monarch.

Units of measure

Coins

The monetary system differs from country to country. Most countries use a system of slim, tubular clay beads that can be strung on a thread or a throng. The values vary according to their marking, thus they are called markers. Metals such as bronze, copper, brass and silver are also shaped into beads. Without marking, these are usually referred to by the name of the metal. The only metal that is coined is gold. The coins are known as Pentacles in Pelopnos, Abruzzi and all the city-states of Ticino, as Disks elsewhere in Eubonia, and as Dinar on the southern continent.

Time

Time is measured by the disappearance of the sun and the progression of the planets around the "mortal" celestial map. This is a very important concept because time varies from plane to plane. In man's realm, the terms day and rotation, or rota, are used interchangeably. The nearest equivalent to a week is a "tenday". The "days of the week" are usually designated by number: Oneday, Twoday, Threeday, etc. The "year" is gauged by the revolution of the five moons and the planets overhead. It is usually referred to as a turn.

Height and weight

Height is measured in handspans and the unit for measuring weight is called simply that: "a weight". A single weight is equivalent to ten imperial pounds or about four and a half kilogrammes.